CAPROCK RANGE

CAPROCK RANGE

Ed La Vanway

GUNSMOKE

First published in the US by Avalon Books

This hardback edition 2012
by AudioGO Ltd
by arrangement with
Golden West Literary Agency

ISBN 978 1 445 82418 5

British Library Cataloguing in Publication Data available.

Printed and bound in Great Britain by
MPG Books Group Limited

Ed La Vanway was an author whose life remains shrouded in mystery. His career as a Western writer began in 1948 with the appearance of the short story, "Deadlocked" in *Triple Western* (4/48), and ended with publication of his fifth Western novel, *Gunfire Mountain* (Avalon Books, 1962). During these fourteen years he moved frequently around Bakersfield, California. He had several different addresses within a short space of time and then all correspondence between this author and his agent ceased in 1963. In 1956 La Vanway had become a member of the Western Writers of America but he supplied the organization with no biographical information and so there was no write-up of him in the WWA house publication *The Roundup* which customarily was done to showcase accomplishments and past publications of new members. In his two novels published by Dodd, Mead, no biography appeared in the books, only a notice that the author was a member of the Western Writers of America. His membership in the WWA was not renewed in 1963. He had never attended a convention and no member could recall ever having met him. If Ed La Vanway had died, there was no obituary in any newspaper and research conducted by the staff at the Beale Memorial Library in Bakersfield could not find any telephone listing for Ed La Vanway from 1944 to 1963, and he is not buried in any of the county cemeteries. If La Vanway did not die in 1963, he quite definitely did disappear. Yet what is of overriding importance about this author is the impressive quality of the Western fiction he produced in those fourteen years. With every event and development in his stories it is as if the options are always kept open, so that a reader never knows what is going to happen, and, when things do happen, they always come as something of a surprise and are handled with an uncommon adroitness. While all of La Vanway's Western fiction is well worth reading, truly extraordinary examples would certainly be *The Brand Rider* (Dodd, Mead, 1958), and among his twenty-five magazine stories, "No Wedding for the Wild One" in *Western Novel and Short Stories* (1/56). A La Vanway story is always a special occasion.

CHAPTER I

Daylight was breaking by the time breakfast was over, and the Bar G *remudero* was hazing in the cavvy. Most of the hands headed for the corral to saddle up. Rufe Tolliver stopped to roll a smoke, and the foreman said to him, "You and Sprague seem to hit it off all right, Tolliver. Go with him this morning and pull bog along that stretch of—"

Tolliver was shaking his head.

Kelse's eyes widened in surprise. He was a hefty big-boned man with a heavy jaw and close-set eyes under a bulging brow and a low-pulled hat. His beefy shoulders were encased in a jacket of brown duck.

"Are you having a difficulty with Walt Sprague, too?"

"I get along with him. Fact is, if he was foreman here, I might not even be quitting—some of the others would. I know the difference between cowhands and gun-slingers, Kelse."

Kelse stared at him in narrow speculation. "Ben

won't like you to quit. You figure to go up to your place?"

"I'm thinking about it."

Kelse glanced toward the corral and said, "Ben figured you'd forget that idea after you'd been with us awhile."

"I've got my last-year's wages invested in that claim. I'm going to make a cattle ranch out of it."

Kelse reflected. "Well," he said, "you won't have to fight Injuns now, like the other fellow did, but you won't be able to run cattle up there, not to amount to anything. Ben won't let you. You can't even get to it without trespassing on Bar G graze."

"That's just your opinion. And Ben Gregory's."

"Figure you can take Lurelle up there and hide behind her skirts?" Kelse asked, sneering.

"I don't see why I ought to tell you my plans."

A long-jawed man with sandy hair, Tolliver had been with this Bar G outfit only four months, not long enough to pile up as big a grubstake as he needed but he and Lurelle had decided it was time for him to leave, before he became involved in her father's fight with the Muleshoe spread.

Tolliver considered himself a Texan, but he had been born in South Carolina, his family migrating to Austin when he was too young to remember the move. During the Rebellion, he had served with Thirty-second Regiment of Texas Cavalry, and after Appomattox he had drifted.

He had come to this valley of the Dragoon from the South Concho country as a trail hand last October with a herd of she-stuff Ben Gregory had bargained for, and then he had bought squatter's rights to an abandoned claim, yonder in the hills to the southeast, instead of going back with his outfit. Having invested nearly all of his savings in a quitclaim deed to the hill place, he'd hired out to Ben Gregory. He had to get some money to repair the run-down buildings.

But actually he had hired on with the Gregory spread because of Ben's daughter, Lurelle.

Tolliver had been across this Dragoon River range a couple of times before, several years back. Liking its looks, and feeling he could get a start here, he'd planned to return someday. Now he was here. He had acquired a start as a cowman, too, if he could hang on to it.

He hadn't branded one critter yet, but there were more maverick cattle without ranches, he told himself, than there were maverick ranches without cattle. He'd get cattle.

Gregory's opposition to Tolliver's plans wasn't a matter of crowded grass. This whole upper valley was occupied by only three ranches. It was controlled by just two, Gregory's Bar G and the Hashims' Muleshoe, yonder across the Dragoon River.

The Dragoon valley was elbow-shaped, a hundred

and seventy miles long, bordered by the plateau country on the north and by the Pecos River in the southwest. Here, the upper part of it ranged from fifteen to twenty-five miles in width. Except for a creek threading through the timbered hills where Tolliver's claim was located, the valley was bordered on either side by waterless sand hills, but this north-south section of the valley contained about seven hundred thousand acres of rich grazing land.

Ben Gregory had settled here with the idea of claiming all of it. Gregory had pioneered this valley, trailing in a herd of longhorn cattle and bringing his household goods and family in ox-drawn covered wagons. He had built this Bar G headquarters in 1866.

In 1868 Morgan Hashim had driven in a herd of longhorns to settle beyond Gregory, across the Dragoon, establishing the Muleshoe spread. He and Hashim had disagreed from the beginning. Gregory was embittered by his own lack of foresight. Now he realized, too late, that he should have built his Bar G headquarters west of the river, where the Hashims had located; then he could have held both that range and this. There was twice as much grazing land on the Muleshoe side of the stream.

The best grass was in the lower part of the valley, but the Lipans and Kickapoos and Comanches had fought harder to keep that and had choused the

Gregorys and the Hashims out of that part, back in the sixties.

In 1872 a settlement had grown up around the stage swing station established at the Dragoon crossing. And now Eagle Bend was a booming town, and Tolliver intended to head for there this morning.

Other cowmen had trailed into the Dragoon country during the past few years, taking up the lower valley. Maybe all the way to the Pecos, as far as Tolliver knew.

There was one other spread in the upper valley that Gregory hadn't wanted here, at first.

Two years ago, Mark Connick, backed by Morgan Hashim, had fitted up a Muleshoe line camp for a ranch headquarters so that he could start his Circle C brand. Hashim was about to lose some of his lower range to Ben Gregory, valley people said, and had put Connick there to keep Gregory off. Hashim would rather see an outsider get the graze than be crowded off by Gregory.

No one knew much about Connick, except that his father had been Morgan Hashim's business associate, back in Kentucky.

Last year, Morgan had been bushwhacked on the Eagle Bend trail. The Muleshoe was now being run by his sons, Lee and Cliff, and according to what Tolliver had heard, the younger Hashims were even more determined to wipe out Ben Gregory than their father had been.

It had reached the point where it couldn't go on much longer, Lurelle said.

Tolliver wanted to tell her it would go on forever, that only people died; the thing behind human passion did not. But he just listened without comment to Lurelle.

She was heartsick about the trouble between the two families, and longed to start her own family off with a clean slate.

Lurelle had known instantly, it seemed, that Rufe Tolliver was the man to head her family—if she could prevent his throwing in with her father against the Hashims. And she was succeeding. Something inside Tolliver told him to listen closely to what Ben's daughter had to say.

This was the reason he confronted Kelse now. . . .

Breath fogging in the chill of early morning, the big foreman said surlily, "Well, you'll have to ask for your time yourself. I won't do it for you."

He started toward the corral. Suddenly changing his mind, he turned and came back. Staring hostilely at Tolliver for a moment, he said, "We'll find out just what's what about you. Stick around." Spurs clanking, he went toward the ranch house.

"Ben wants to see you, Tolliver," he said when he came back. "Go around to the front."

Gregory himself answered Tolliver's rap—a grizzled man of medium build, fifty years old. His hair was close-cropped, eyebrows stiff, mustache short and bristly. A savage temper had cut deep lines in his face, and his mouth was down-curved. He led the way into the living room but didn't continue on into the ranch office. He told Tolliver to take a chair.

"Kelse tells me you ain't satisfied here."

"I like it here all right, Ben. Pretty tough outfit, some of them, but they don't bother me. It's just that I have plans of my own. When I hired out to you, I didn't know you wanted to use my gun against the Muleshoe. You sized me up wrong."

"No sand in your craw?"

"I've always gotten by, Ben."

Gregory's mustached lip curled. "I sized you up right, Tolliver. I figured you was just a saddle tramp looking for somebody to feed you and let you lay around all winter. I knew all the time you'd run out when the sap got to running."

"Don't chew me out, Ben. Just hand me my pay."

"You got no pay coming."

Tolliver watched him wryly. "Why haven't I? I've been here four months and haven't seen the color of your money yet."

"You've eaten hearty. That ought to satisfy you— loafed around all winter and stuffed your gut three times a day."

"Ben, you know I've made you a hand. I've been

half-frozen all winter long. And you're going to pay me for the work I've done here. If you don't, you'll be sorry for it."

"You'll rustle my cattle to start your two-bit ranch?"

"I won't steal from you."

Gregory shook his head. "No, you won't steal from me. You haven't got the guts to. The Lerda gang hasn't got guts enough to rustle Bar G stuff. You ain't been here long, Tolliver, but you know how I treat cow thieves."

Tolliver offered no comment.

"Are you really going up to your squatter place, or are you aiming to hire out to the Muleshoe for more money?"

"They wouldn't hire a saddle tramp, would they?"

"You're a killer. You've been making your living that way, or you wouldn't be giving them hands of mine so much lip."

"Ben, I told you I'm no professional gun-slinger."

"Better be telling it straight. If you start working for my enemies now, after I took care of you all winter, I'll put a bounty on your ears, one at a time."

"Don't threaten me, Ben. If I decide to work for the Muleshoe, I'll do it. Pay me what I've got coming."

Gregory shook his head. "We're square, up to now. Roll your soogans, and get. Or I'll turn Kelse loose on you."

White around the mouth, Tolliver gathered up his hat and stood erect. Gregory rose to his feet.

"I'll go. But get ready to swap hide with me."

Gregory lifted a clenched fist and almost hit Tolliver, but then he turned away muttering, "Ah, go on."

Tolliver caught up his horse and saddled it and led it over to the bunkhouse, tying his bedroll behind the cantle. Afterward, he went to the cookshack for some chuck to eat on the trail. He didn't get any. He asked for some salt. The cook refused.

Tolliver turned to the stove, looking for a kettle of something to dump on the floor. It wasn't actually the grub or the salt; it was the cook's siding with Kelse against him that angered Tolliver, because the foreman had been in here saying not to give Tolliver anything. Tolliver didn't touch any of the kettles; the cook had a sudden change of heart and poured him some salt, about enough to fill a cigarette paper.

Lurelle had glanced into the cookshack during the argument. When Tolliver returned to the bunkhouse, he found her standing near his horse, and she had come out into the morning's chill wearing only a housecoat. She was a tall girl, with shining black hair. Her eyes were dark and long-lashed and filled now with concern.

"Sometimes Ben doesn't sleep well," she said, "and he's cross as a bear early of a morning."

"He says I'm leaving right when the work is starting. He wouldn't pay me, so I can't go to the claim now, Lurelle."

Her brows knit. "He'll pay you."

"I don't think so. It's best to let it ride for now."

"If you're broke, let me—"

He cut her a quick look, for that part of it had already been thrashed out. A new start, he'd told her, meant getting started through their own efforts—not on money Ben had given her.

"I'll get a temporary job until I can collect from Ben."

"Don't fall for those big wages over at the Muleshoe."

Tolliver cut another quick glance at her. "Serve Ben right if I did, after him trying to throw a scare into me. Now he'll be bragging to everybody about how I knuckled under and rode off with my tail between my legs. But he's your father, and I wouldn't do anything against him. You know that."

Tolliver turned to tighten his saddle cinches and heard men shout from the back gallery, "Lurelle, come back in here and get some clothes on. Too cold to be down there thataway."

Watching Tolliver, Lurelle said, "I'll bet he would pay you right now if you'd go back up there."

"But I won't go. He'll bring it to me the next time."

Lurelle stood there, pretty features sorely

troubled. When Tolliver was ready to leave, she said, in a choked tone, "I can't tell you good-by," and hurried toward the house.

Tolliver swung astride his roan.

CHAPTER II

The wind blew all day long and the sky was overcast, occasionally spitting flurries of snow, and Tolliver rode down long grassy flats with an eye out for meat. He also sized up the cattle he passed, his plans for a future here and his cowhand upbringing making him deeply interested in how well the longhorns had wintered. The Bar G stuff had done well, had kept their fat. This was fine range the year around, this valley of the Dragoon. All of it.

Late in the afternoon Tolliver rode to a grassy clearing. Using his catch-rope, he staked the roan out and started still-hunting with his carbine. He had gone a half-mile downriver before he shot a fat buck. He bled the carcass, then went back to get his horse, to pitch camp where he had shot the deer, and he almost lost the buck to a pack of wolves. Driving them away; he built a fire and began broiling venison steaks, and the wolves kept trotting around him in the timber, frightening his horse.

They were gaunt, ribby varmints, and Tolliver

actually felt sorry for them. Winter had forced them down from the high country. Tolliver cussed them. "Head for the buffalo range, you fools. Meat going to waste there right now, and you ought to be getting your part of it."

The roan continued to tremble with instinctive revulsion, so Tolliver decided not to camp for the night. Besides, he had no coffee, and figured to ride on to the settlement and have a cup. He left the deer meat for the varmints and reached Eagle Bend just before daybreak.

Only the Bar G outfit used the trail he had come down. Part of the way it was the trail from his own place, but Tolliver reached town without having met another rider.

Like many other southwestern towns, Eagle Bend had sprung up around a plaza laid out among giant old live oaks. Tolliver rode to the center of the square to water his horse and to scrub himself at the trough.

The big general store, the bank, and the barber shop were in darkness, but the Desert Star Saloon was open for business. lights were burning in the office of the Plaza Feed and Sale Stable and in the restaurant and bakery. There were lights also in the big adobe hotel, stage station and express office. The Brass Rail Saloon, a saddlery and Sheriff Jim Stroud's home and office stood north of the square.

The sheriff's home and office was a red-tile-roofed adobe behind a head-high adobe fence. All the county business was transacted there, for this county still had neither courthouse nor jail. Stroud was compelled to escort vicious prisoners to the lockup in San Angelo, in Tom Green County—compelled by conscience, that was, for every now and then Stroud took into custody a man, even though vicious, who was deemed worthy of the spark of life. The others were shot or hanged before Jim Stroud got to them officially.

Stroud never bothered the Lerda gang, though.

There were small homes of adobe and log on the north, behind the business structures, and others on the east. Those on the east, back of the Desert Star Saloon, were where the Lerda gang holed up when in Eagle Bend.

Tolliver had kept clear of the Lerda gang so far and intended to stay clear of them. When anyone visited this settlement, however, he was always conscious that it was a Lerda town.

Mounting, Tolliver jogged across to the liveryman's and made arrangements to stable his horse on credit. Then, shouldering his bedroll, he went over to the hotel and rented a room, also on credit.

He was as angry at himself as at Ben Gregory now. Why hadn't he made Ben pay him? Afraid of Kelse and Jepsen and those other fellows? That was the way it looked. Well, Ben would pay him soon, he vowed.

Ben was a range-hog. And the Hashims were no better.

Nowadays, with the West settling up, no one ranch had the right to claim a chunk of state land measuring a two-day ride, end to end. That was how the pioneer cowmen had done. They'd claimed all the land within sight of the spot they had settled on, and served notice they intended to hold it.

Some of them had gone about buying up enough land certificates to acquire court title to their holdings. That, too, in some instances, had been high-handed thievery, and many a title had changed hands because of a whipsaw fight with the authorities and bogus-certificate locators.

The authorities had to be crooked, of course, to connive in such land steals, but Texas, since the days of Moses, had had almost as many double-dealing politicians as longhorn cattle. This valley of the Dragoon would see a showdown court fight someday, when the government surveyors came, and Tolliver wondered if the Bar G and the Muleshoe would survive. Instead of being at each other's throats, the Gregorys and the Hashims ought to get together and double-team against those land locators. But no matter what happened, no one was going to chouse Tolliver off his claim in the Dragoon Hills. He had a quitclaim to it, and could hang onto it the way the Gregory and the Hashim clans had so far kept theirs.

Tolliver slept until afternoon and then dug a clean shirt and pants and socks out of his warbag. He put on a fringed jacket, buckled on his gun belt and canted his hat, and went down onto the hotel veranda. The town, even at this hour, looked none too busy. Not more than twenty saddle horses were in sight, and no rigs at all.

Landing a job, therefore, might prove difficult.

Tolliver headed toward the *barberia*, deciding to break his last gold piece. He listened to the music and revelry from the Desert Star Saloon while he was getting shaved. After that he went across the plaza for a meal at the restaurant; then, as he had never cared to mix with the crowd in the Desert Star, he entered the Brass Rail.

There were a dozen customers in the place, teamsters and army men and cowhands. Tolliver took a chair, listened to the talk, and while looking at a Dodge City newspaper, he felt eyes upon him.

He tossed the paper aside, glanced idly around and then looked at the man watching him. Dressed in expensive range garb, the fellow was broad of shoulders, heavy of build, with a darkly tanned face, blue eyes and a thick shock of cowlicked yellow hair. Tolliver got to his feet, straightening his gun harness, and walked over to the bar.

The yellow-haired man grinned. "Have a drink?"

"Thanks, but I'm stuffed to the gills," Tolliver

said. "You know the old saying—'no whisky on a full stomach, or food in an empty one.' "

"Take a cigar, then." The man pulled one from his vest.

After they had lighted up, the man extended his hand. "I'm Chet Bigelow—cattle buyer."

"My name's Tolliver. Afraid I can't help you any."

Bigelow nodded. "I've heard your name spoken. You've got some cattle for sale, haven't you? Somebody told me you had a sizable herd of steers up there in those Dragoon Hills."

Tolliver shook his head, watching the yellow-haired man through cigar smoke. "I don't know why they keep that rumor going. I've got a small place up there. No cattle yet. I'll be buying some she-stuff myself before too long."

Bigelow's bland countenance became shrewd and calculating. "I don't care what they are. Or what brand they're wearing."

Tolliver grimaced. He dropped Bigelow's cigar, mashing it with a high-heeled boot. He looked up, saying dourly, "Told you I didn't have any cattle. I won't ever have any for you. Man buys a critter from me, he won't have to guard it because of its brand. I'll guarantee that."

Bigelow's features relaxed and his grin returned. "I'm talking cattle, man, not looking for a fight with you."

One thing Tolliver knew for certain: Bigelow wasn't a bit afraid to hunt trouble. From the man's appearance, he would fight anybody.

Going out onto the saloon porch, Tolliver pushed Bigelow from his mind, having no time at all for anyone who was willing to deal in stolen stock.

As he stood there, jingling the change from his double eagle, he thought, Damn Ben Gregory. If Ben had paid him, Tolliver could have loaded up with supplies and headed for his own place. If Ben . . .

Recalling that one of the cowhands inside the saloon had mentioned his boss was looking for bronc stompers, Tolliver went back for more information. He was getting a little old for bronc busting, but he needed only a temporary job. Well, it was sure temporary—a man couldn't stand much of it at a time. It would pay, though, and Tolliver wanted his grubstake to add up in a hurry.

Tolliver was gone from Eagle Bend for two months and rode back onto the public square on a warm day in May. When he drew rein at the Plaza corral, Sheriff Jim Stroud came from his office to ask, "Where have you been, Tolliver?" The lawman was a paunchy, flat-faced fellow with thin blond hair plastered to his forehead. His interest in Tolliver seemed to have increased considerably during Tolliver's absence.

"Down the river, Sheriff, breaking horses."

"Couldn't get along with Ben Gregory, huh?"

Tolliver shook his head.

"Guess you heard about the Hashim boys getting killed?"

The hostler took Tolliver's roan, and Tolliver told him to pull the bedroll off the saddle, then turned again to the sheriff. "Gun fight or a dry-gulching?"

Stroud wiped his chin and looked furtive for a brief moment but then said with professional finality, "A running gun fight. Happened on their own Muleshoe range. Ben didn't take part in it. He came and got me and I went up there and looked around —he didn't go over to the Muleshoe with me. Phillips and Sturdivant told me the boys' guns had been emptied. Nothing I could do about it. Long trip for me, too, and I won't get any mileage out of it."

Tolliver kept his expression inscrutable.

"I sure feel sorry for Fanny," Stroud continued. "Husband gone. Sons gone. Just her and Cheryl. What on earth will they do? What are you aiming to do now, Tolliver?"

Tolliver turned away for a moment, frowning. He glanced back to say, "Go up to my place, I reckon."

"Want that Muleshoe foreman job?"

"No, I sure don't."

"What's the matter? Don't want to work for the Muleshoe on account of Lurelle? Your sympathies are all with the Bar G, eh?"

"When I quit Ben Gregory, Sheriff, I couldn't even collect the pay I had coming."

"And couldn't make a fuss about it either, on account of the gal?"

"That's right."

The sheriff chuckled without mirth. "Knowing Ben, I'd say you might never get it. Well, Lurelle's worth it, I'd figure. She sure thinks a lot of Ben, but he don't deserve it. Lurelle's like her ma, I hear. Ben's woman sure must have been a fine lady. But she'd passed on before I came here. Lurelle's here now. Moved to town. Working for Allenthorp."

Tolliver stared. "Funny she'd do that."

"Ben says she followed you here."

"Ben's liable to say anything."

"I'll say it myself—she did follow you here."

Tolliver shrugged. He said, "When are you going to collar the man who bushwhacked Morgan Hashim, Sheriff?"

"I'm still working on it."

"Ben do it?" Tolliver watched him intently.

"I wouldn't put it past him. Ben might have hired it done." Stroud was thoughtfully silent, then said, "Ah, we probably won't ever know who's guilty of that killing. Now, how about going to work for Fanny Hashim, Tolliver?"

Tolliver shook his head and turned around, looking toward the Desert Star Saloon. He saw two men on the porch, one of them a leader of the renegades who holed up in the *jacales* behind the building.

The Lerda gang was one of Stroud's biggest worries, Tolliver knew. But Tolliver was aware that so long as the Lerdas were quiet in Stroud's bailiwick and weren't specifically wanted by some other peace officer, Stroud wouldn't lift a warrant against them. And Tolliver didn't blame him.

The man standing with Bill Lerda on the saloon porch was old Jake Mawson, a stove-up old cowpuncher.

"Bad blood between them two," Stroud said speculatively. "They've been fussing ever since Scott left."

"Where did Scott go?"

"Dodge City. A trail herd was stampeded down on Devils River and a thousand head lost. Several men were killed. Putting two and two together, I'd say Scott Lerda's got them. He's been gone long enough now to be back. Guess he had trouble finding a buyer. How'll he get shut of cattle without a bill of sale or inspection papers? You've been up to railhead?"

"Yeah. There's always a few shady buyers tied in with a crooked packing house. Scott won't have trouble. But he could have sold that herd right here, to a big yellow-haired—Bigelow, that's his name."

"You're joking," Stroud said. He was smiling.

"Well, he sure tried to buy some stolen cattle off

of me. He'd just as soon deal with Scott and Bill
Lerda, wouldn't he?"

Smile broadening, Stroud said, "Sooner."

Resentful, Tolliver said, "This is the first range I
was ever on where they mistook me for a rustler. Bigelow's not the only one. Everybody's saying that's what
I'm doing with that place in the hills—holding stolen
cattle there."

"I'm not saying it," the sheriff told him, sober-
ing.

Tolliver smiled. "I know that, Jim." He took off
his hat and slapped dust from his clothes.

Sheriff Stroud said, "Come over to the house after
a while and let's talk about that Muleshoe job, Tolliver. Might turn into something a damned sight better than a greasy-sack outfit up there in them Dragoon Hills."

Tolliver deliberated. He didn't want to work for
the Muleshoe, but he didn't want to give Jim
Stroud a direct refusal either. Stroud was putting it
to him pretty hard. Almost any man, unless he kept
his guard up, would feel sorry for a couple of women
trying to hang onto a ranch the size of the Muleshoe
at a time like this, when an influx of newcomers hope-
fully eyed every blade of grass that sprouted.

First of all, though, Tolliver intended to see
Lurelle. He told Stroud so, saying then, "I'll be at
your place in a couple of hours. How's that?"

"I'll be right there waiting for you," Stroud said. He didn't try to hide his relief.

After he left, Tolliver wondered if Stroud's tone hadn't held more than relief. The sheriff had actually sounded desperate. Why so? Stroud would draw his pay, no matter what happened to the Muleshoe. Or to the Bar G, either.

CHAPTER III

Tolliver carried his bedroll to the hotel and regis-
tered, noticing that Fanny Hashim and her daughter Cheryl were in town. Changing clothes, Tolliver speculated as to their presence here, for they
had been in town several days. Usually they stayed
no more than one night.

Sheriff Stroud was trying to hire a foreman for
Fanny Hashim. Maybe that was it—Fanny was here
to hire hands. Gun hands. She was getting set now
for an all-out war with Ben Gregory and the hard-
case bunch of gun-slingers he'd tried to palm off on
Tolliver as cowhands.

So that's why Stroud was so interested in his taking
the Muleshoe job. The sheriff's real opinion of him
was the same as Ben Gregory's—a killer for hire.

Putting on his best pants, Tolliver brushed the
dust from his boots, and when he went downstairs,
he walked toward Allenthorp's Mercantile.

There were five men on the porch of the general store, four of them buffalo hunters, come to Eagle

Bend to see the sights, play poker, drink whisky, and get their heads busted open.

The fifth man was the fellow who'd turned a Muleshoe line shack into a headquarters for his Circle C iron—Mark Connick.

Connick was tall and erect, with dark hair and a black mustache. His eyes were dark brown, sharp. Under a flat-crowned light hat, his face was young looking, and he was wearing a suit of store clothes with a cartridge belt showing across his middle. The tip of his holster hung below his coat.

Tolliver was wary of him—for one reason. Although set up in the cattle business by Morgan Hashim, Connick had tried to shine up to Lurelle Gregory and was still trying to. That was double-crossing the Hashims, actually. So Connick wasn't the type of man Tolliver would trust, or turn his back to.

But the Bar G and the Muleshoe both were claiming far too much range, and a man longing to get started for himself found it difficult to hold either range-hog outfit in high regard.

As Tolliver came up the steps of Allenthorp's Mercantile, Connick moved over to stand in the double doorway. He said, "Ben wants you to keep away from her, Tolliver."

"That won't stop me from seeing her."

"Let her alone, Tolliver. She's mine. I intend to marry her."

"I'll ask her about it."

Connick made a left-handed gesture of impatience. "I didn't mean it was all cut and dried. Ben claims that the only reason she came to town was to learn something of your whereabouts. What did you say to her that turned her head like that?"

Connick's earnest concern dispelled Tolliver's tension. His mouth relaxed. Suddenly he found pleasure in the thought that Lurelle couldn't stay up there on the Bar G without him.

"We almost had her in the notion of going home," Connick continued, "but if she sees you, she won't do it. She ought to. Lurelle hasn't got any business staying in town."

"She won't stay long."

"She's using bad judgment," Connick said. "Ben's rich. She'll get it all someday, unless she turns him against her."

"By encouraging me?"

Connick nodded.

"Maybe she'd rather have me than Ben's money."

Connick looked scornful. "Lurelle won't ever marry you. Ben won't let her. If he had tightened down on her, she wouldn't have come to town at all. He didn't want to hurt her feelings. You're the one he's going to hold responsible."

"You aim to help him?"

Connick's eyes narrowed.

"Get out of the way," Tolliver said softly, and as Connick stepped aside, Tolliver turned into the store.

Allenthorp's Mercantile was a big establishment, the retail part of it a huge room filled with stacks and shelves of goods hauled down from the Kansas railroad. Rows of hams and shoulders hung from hooks. Harness and water buckets and washtubs were suspended from the ceiling beams. Barrels of vinegar and flour and sugar stood about, and huge hogsheads of molasses. Racks of axes and shovels and other tools, and buggy whips with kegs of nails and horseshoes were rowed in the center. All of it smelled of spices and leather and woollen goods.

Half a dozen clerks were busy with customers.

Tolliver could see the full length of the building. Lurelle was out on the loading dock in back. When he came near, she glanced around, and a happy light sprang into her eyes.

Tolliver touched his hat. "How are you?" he asked.

Lurelle was checking merchandise as clerks trundled it out of the wareroom to load into the back-action wagon of a jerkline freight outfit, bound for a ranch in the lower valley.

"I'm fine," Lurelle murmured.

"Don't you know your father is one of the richest cowmen in Texas?"

"You know how he got that way? By working. I'm

learning things a ranch woman needs to know. When I buy my supplies now, I'll bet I get my money's worth."

"Yes, I know that. But this is a rough town."

Lurelle looked at him. "Anybody gets rough with me, I'll get rough with them. You just don't know me, Rufe."

"If you've got a mean streak," he said, "I ain't ever seen it. If I had known you were in town with nobody to keep an eye on you, I'd have worried my head off."

Her features became sober, and he knew she was thinking of marriage. Lurelle expected him to ask her to marry him right now, so that she could move onto the hill place with him. At this moment she was his for the asking. Yet, something held him silent.

She smiled. "I had someone to keep an eye on me, mister."

"Connick?"

"Yes, Connick. But I meant Sheriff Stroud. Felicia wouldn't let me stay at the hotel, so I moved into one of her rooms. I've been eating at the restaurant."

"Didn't quarrel with Ben, did you, when you left home?"

"Heavens, no."

"Ben doesn't like your being here."

She shook her head, and was busy checking sales slips.

"Could I see you tonight?"

"Sure. Come by at eight, and we'll eat together."

Tolliver took leave of Lurelle then, inwardly troubled. He bought cartridges and smoking tobacco on his way through the store.

The buffalo hunters were gone, but Mark Connick was leaning against a tree over on the plaza, as though waiting to intercept Tolliver.

North of the store, in front of the bank, Tolliver noticed a shock of yellow hair under a high-peaked hat, and recognized Bigelow, the cattle buyer. If Bigelow had become a permanent resident, it sure hadn't helped Eagle Bend any.

A couple of Mexicans were squatting on either side of the swinging doors of the Desert Star Saloon, arms folded on knees and tall sombreros pointing horizontally as they bowed their heads in siesta that was probably feigned.

Bill Lerda had stationed the pair there as lookouts, and he had ordered them to watch Bigelow. Knowing that Bigelow handled considerable money, Lerda was no doubt interested in the fellow's comings and goings from the bank.

Tolliver watched Lerda emerge from the barber shop. He cut a quick glance toward the general store, and for an instant Tolliver thought he would get whipsawed, Connick coming at him from one direction, Lerda from another. Then he remembered that there was bad blood between the Lerda brothers and Mark Connick.

The reason for it, Tolliver had heard, was that Connick, when he first came to the valley, had publicly stated he'd recognized Bill and Scott Lerda among a band of road agents who'd held up the stage he was riding in, near Weatherford. But now, for whatever cause, Connick was arrantly afraid of them.

Lerda was about the same age as Tolliver. He had a thick-lipped mouth and a wide nose, and was chunky of build. He had killed a man shortly before Tolliver's arrival in Eagle Bend. According to all who knew him, Bill was snake-mean, but not as mean as the younger one, Scott.

Tolliver stood there a moment mulling over what Sheriff Stroud had told him—Scott had trailed a herd of stolen longhorns to Dodge City. Why hadn't Bigelow bought that herd? Well, maybe Bigelow hadn't been here at the time.

Lerda put his back to Tolliver, heading for the Desert Star Saloon, and Tolliver stepped toward the square.

Connick was still leaning against the biggest oak, near the water trough. Wood shavings lay thick at his feet. Closing his clasp knife, he straightened as Tolliver came up, and Tolliver said to him, "Still got something in your craw?"

"Did you tell Lurelle to go home?"

Tolliver just looked at him.

"Ask her to marry you?" Connick asked.

"No, but I will."

Connick's face showed contempt. "When you get enough change to buy some beans to feed her on?"

Frowning, Tolliver studied him. "What are you trying to do, fellow?"

"Marry Lurelle. And you're in my way. Why don't you rattle your hocks?"

"Any leaving done, you'll do it."

Connick shrugged. "Ben'll take care of you. Ben Gregory eats out of my hand."

Tolliver said, "Because you bushwhacked Morgan Hashim for him."

Connick glanced around, seeing that no one else was within earshot. He nodded. "Just between you and me," he said, a dark eyebrow going up, "that's exactly why."

Tolliver's face contorted with disgust. "Morgan Hashim set you up in the cattle business and then you plugged him in the back. What kind of a double-crossing skunk are you?"

"Morgan had it coming. He looked at Cheryl and me like Ben looks at you and Lurelle. Ordered me to keep away from her. Thought she was too good for me and said I was getting too big for my britches. He claimed he would see me in hell before he would let me have her." Connick paused; then he added morosely, "I've changed my mind now. I wouldn't have Cheryl Hashim at all. I want Lurelle."

Tolliver said, "You won't get her. I won't see you in hell, but I'll sure put you there."

With a slight nod of his head, Connick said, "Maybe you'll get what Morgan got."

Tolliver leaned sidewise to spit, saying afterward, "You're after the Bar G, Connick. You don't care anything about Lurelle. If you did accidentally win her, Ben Gregory's life won't be worth much."

Connick's manner became persuasively business-like. "You've got it all figured out, Tolliver—just like I thought. And that's why I waited here to talk with you. I want the Bar G and the Muleshoe, too. If all the upper valley was turned into one ranch, the way Ben planned it, a man could hold it against all comers—make it the finest spread in West Texas."

"Better keep your plans to yourself," Tolliver said.

"Wait. Both of us know that you're really the only gun in this valley dangerous to me. I can ease out of my difficulty with the Lerdas. And if you'll just hold still, I'll make it worth your while. I can't do it now. but—"

For an instant Tolliver considered knocking Connick down, but he said, "Be right interesting to see how you make out."

Connick's sharp gaze didn't waver. Presently, he walked toward the Brass Rail Saloon. Tolliver went on across the square for a late dinner.

CHAPTER IV

Over in New Mexico, some years before moving to Texas and running for sheriff of this county, Jim Stroud had married into a wealthy Spanish-American family, and his present home near the northwest corner of the square, Tolliver supposed, was owned by his wife's people. It was a far more pretentious place than Stroud could have built with his salary, although he probably drew rent from the county for its use as an office and courtroom.

There was an ornamental iron gate in the adobe fence. The front yard was narrow and barren, and there was just an adobe wall that lifted to a short, steeply pitched roof, with iron-barred windows on either side of an arched passageway.

Entering this passage, Tolliver continued on toward the patio where four children were playing, the offspring of Jim and Felicia Stroud. One of the youngsters was a diapered toddler and the oldest was about nine, Tolliver judged.

A spring flowed in the center of the enclosure, filling a rock-lined water-lily pool. Doors around the patio gave into the various apartments, one of which was occupied by Lurelle Gregory.

The children, intent on some kind of a jumping game and accustomed to frequent callers, paid Tolliver no mind. No one else seemed to be about.

Suddenly then a girl's voice was raised in an outburst of tearful anger, saying, "No!" and Tolliver turned toward an open door.

Sheriff Stroud was in that room. Upon seeing Tolliver, whom he had been expecting, he stepped out into the patio. The lawman was bareheaded, thin hair plastered to his scalp. His flat face was glum.

"It's Cheryl Hashim, Tolliver. She's upset and mad —mad at her ma—and I can't say as I blame her." The sheriff turned back, motioning for Tolliver to enter the room.

Tolliver did so, removing his hat. Besides the Hashim girl, a buxom Mexican woman, mother of the four children, was in the room.

Stroud said, "You've met my wife, haven't you, Tolliver?

Tolliver said, "Howdy, ma'am. Yes, we've met, Sheriff."

"You came here weeth Don Ramon and Ben Gregory to get a bill of sale weetnessed."

"You have a good memory. That was quite a while back."

She sobered. Both she and her husband put their attention on the Hashim girl.

The room was furnished as a sitting room and bedroom, and Cheryl was reclining in a deep armchair. She was slender but well-rounded, a handsome girl with reddish-brown hair, a pretty mouth and deep brown eyes. Her mouth was unsteady now, however, and her eyes were red and swollen from weeping.

Sheriff Stroud spoke to her gruffly. "Stop that taking-on now, Cheryl. Tolliver's going to have a little talk with Bill about you."

Tolliver cut the badge-toter a startled, angry look.

"What good will that do?" the girl asked tearfully. "He can't talk to Mama."

"Me and Tolliver both can talk to her. We'll make her come to her senses. Just forget it, because you haven't got anything at all to worry about now."

Cheryl sat there for a minute with a faraway look in her eyes and then began crying again, silently.

Tolliver's eyes contained a cornered look. He wanted to ask what was wrong between Cheryl and Fanny Hashim. He wanted to ask about Bill—if it was Bill Lerda. It was plain, however, that Stroud didn't want to be questioned.

It was obvious, also, that Tolliver was being drawn into something not to his liking—the job as foreman of the Muleshoe ranch. Stroud was using this girl's tears to force Tolliver to pick up the Hashims' feud with Ben Gregory—running the risk of having Mark Connick bushwhack him. Or even Ben himself. Ben wanted Tolliver's scalp, anyway, for tolling Lurelle off down here to the settlement. If he took the Muleshoe job, on top of that, he wouldn't last as long as a firefly's wink. And Ben had already given him fair warning.

Jim Stroud was just taking a hell of a lot for granted.

The sheriff picked up his hat and turned to Felicia, saying, "Me and Tolliver will be gone for a while. Get Cheryl into some cooler clothes. Make her get some sleep. If she can't, give her a dose of laudanum."

Felicia nodded.

Stroud jerked his finger, telling Tolliver to come on, and they stepped out into the patio, Tolliver's features hard and his eyes smoky. When they had moved away from the door, the sheriff stopped walking. He looked toward the children.

"See those young ones yonder, Tolliver?"

Tolliver glanced at the sheriff in puzzlement.

"If it wasn't for them kids," Stroud said, "I wouldn't be calling on you for help. I wouldn't call on nobody for help. But I never realized before that a family man doesn't belong to himself. When he butts into trouble that might cost his life, he's really risking something that belongs to his youngsters. Me and Felicia and the children will go back over in New

Mexico and run cattle on a little ranch she owns over there, and forget about law work."

"What kind of help are you talking about?"

But Stroud gave no immediate reply.

They walked on and turned into the *sala*. All the furniture in this room, Tolliver noticed again, was heavy and old. The plaster walls were hung with religious mementos put there by Felicia. Animal pelts were scattered about the floor.

Stroud's office, in a corner of the room, consisted of a hardwood table flanked by ten Windsor chairs —where the justice of the peace and the circuit judge held hearings—a roll-top desk with pigeonholes stuffed with papers, and a swivel chair and a rack of guns. No wanted dodgers were in sight, Stroud's concern being only with the men he himself wanted.

By swiveling around in his chair, Stroud kept Tolliver in sight, and said, "Cheryl is taking on thataway because Bill Lerda attacked her."

"What have you done about it?" Tolliver asked.

"Nothing, yet."

"Well, get up from there and let's go do something."

"Hold on. Let me tell you about it, Tolliver. I can't arrest him—no charge filed against him. I got just as mad as you about it. Maybe a damned sight madder, because I started out to pass word among the cow outfits to take him out and lynch him. That wouldn't work, though. The whole town knows the details.

It's one of them open secrets. Fanny would have to be strung up, too, and a woman hasn't ever been hanged in Texas, to my recollection."

Gaunt features showing disbelief, Tolliver said, "Are you trying to tell me Fanny was in on it—Cheryl's own ma?"

Stroud nodded. He said, "When the Bar G killed Fanny's sons, Tolliver, it did something to her. She took it ten times harder than Morgan's being shot. Now she's made a deal with Bill Lerda. Hired him as foreman of the Muleshoe. Told him when Ben Gregory was dead, he could have a half-interest in the ranch. Cheryl goes with it. I reckon Bill just got over-curious about what he was getting."

"Cheryl tell you that?"

Stroud nodded.

"You really believe it?"

"Don't you—after seeing how she's been bawling?"

"It's true, I guess," Tolliver said. "But Fanny's after the wrong man, Sheriff. Ben isn't the one to set Lerda on. Connick's the fellow she wants. Connick himself told me that he bushwhacked Morgan Hashim, and I'd bet my bottom dollar he had something to do with Fanny's sons getting gunned."

Stroud showed a quick smile of skepticism, and Tolliver could almost read his mind. The sheriff was thinking of the rivalry between Tolliver and Connick for Lurelle, and figuring that Tolliver was just using this chance to get in a lick at his rival.

"I don't think Bill did anything to Cheryl except hug and kiss her," the sheriff said. "Felicia says he didn't. But he will, if he ain't stopped."

"He'll have to be stopped," Tolliver said.

"But how?" Stroud asked worriedly. He paused, then said, "Fanny is plumb wild for revenge. With Bill as foreman of the Muleshoe, she figures she'll be able to drive Ben Gregory out. She thinks that Scott and the rest of the Lerda bunch will help her if Bill is with her. And I'm sure they would.

"I don't know what to do about it," he continued. "I don't aim to get myself killed. The Gregorys and the Hashims were feuding when I came here, and will probably be feuding after I'm gone."

"I don't see how; the Hashim men are all dead. Fanny and Cheryl can't carry on much longer alone."

Stroud said only, "We'll have to move easy. Not arouse folks any more than they're already aroused. I'd hate to see Fanny's good name run down. She was a right nice person before her sons got shot. I believe she sort of figured Morgan was going to get it, sooner or later, but she wasn't looking for them boys to cash in."

"Why pick on me to tell this to?" Tolliver asked.

"Because of the way you feel about Lurelle, and the way she feels about you. You can see the Gregory side of it. I can't. All I can think of is Fanny and Cheryl having to go it alone."

"Well," Tolliver said, "we might talk with Mrs.

Hashim. Try to reason with her. Show her the risk she's taking. If those renegades ever get a toe hold there, they'll beat her out of the Muleshoe."

Stroud said, "I don't aim for Bill to get a toe hold there. I don't aim for him to ever lay hands on Cheryl again." He opened a drawer and took out a silver star. "I'll swear you in as a deputy, Tolliver."

"I don't want to be hampered by a law badge."

Stroud grunted. "When it comes to a matter of life and death, a badge don't hamper me any. Or the law, either. Wear it while we talk with Fanny. She'll pay more attention to us."

When they had crossed the plaza to the hotel, Tolliver found Mark Connick seated in the lobby. Noticing the badge on Tolliver's vest, the Circle C owner said to the sheriff, sarcastically, "Not very particular about who you pin a star on."

"What have you got against Tolliver, except his taking Miss Lurelle away from you?" Stroud taunted.

"Has he?"

"Sure, he has. From the way that gal talks, her and Tolliver are as thick as peas in a pod."

Not liking the conversation, Tolliver said, "Let's go, Sheriff. I've had a bellyful of him already today."

They met Fanny Hashim in the upstairs hallway, on her way to the lobby.

She was a big woman but firmly made, wearing a skirt of brown denim with a dark blouse and a dark range hat. Her hair, once auburn, had turned iron-gray, although she wasn't yet fifty, and her face was tanned and round and smooth. It was her eyes that held Tolliver—sharp, embittered and cynical.

Stroud took off his hat. "Fanny, this here is my new deputy, Rufe Tolliver. You've seen him around—came in here last fall with Don Ramon."

"Yes, I remember seeing him the day Don Ramon told us Ben Gregory had outbid us on that herd. What about him?"

Stroud said, "We came to palaver with you, Fanny. Let's you and me and him set down somewhere."

Mrs. Hashim said, "No use talking to you, Jim Stroud. You don't amount to shucks as law in this valley, and you never have. I don't think your new deputy will, either."

She started toward the stairway.

Tolliver stepped in front of her. "Hold on, ma'am. He's a duly elected law officer; you're imposing on friendship."

It was then that Tolliver noticed the quirt looped to Fanny Hashim's wrist. She drew it up as though to lash him.

"Feel like you want to do it, go ahead, ma'am."

Taking a firmer stand, Stroud said, "Hit him hard, Fanny; then I'll thumb through the books and see what charges I can file against you for resisting an officer of the law."

Mrs. Hashim brought the quirt down sidewise,

slapping her skirt with it. She asked stonily, "What do you want to talk about? Cheryl? What did she tell you, Jim?"

"Me and Felicia together, I reckon she told it all."

Mrs. Hashim stood silent, mouth tight.

"Fanny," the sheriff said wearily, "you're forcing me to do something I don't want to do. If I have to, though, I'll petition the court to take Cheryl away from you."

"You just try it, Jim Stroud!"

"Cheryl's over yonder with Felicia now, crying her eyes out over what Bill Lerda done to her. You think I'll stand for something like that going on in my baili-wick?"

"Cheryl's a little fool. Scared to death of a man. I wonder what she thinks she's made for."

"What do you think?"

"A man, of course."

Stroud shook his head. "Would you bed down with that fellow if you was young again?"

Fanny Hashim stared at him unemotionally.

"You know damned well you wouldn't, Fanny."

Mrs. Hashim shrugged, then turned toward her rooms in the front part of the hotel. Tolliver's quarters were in the rear. He and the sheriff followed Mrs. Hashim into her sitting room, which had two windows and a door opening onto the upper veranda.

Both the upper and lower galleries were arched like arcades and looked down on the San Angelo

New Mexico stage road with its stream of emigrant wagons, army freight outfits, occasional herds of cattle and bands of horses.

Fanny Hashim sank into a chair, her features glum. Stroud sat down beside Tolliver on the couch, asking,

"Closed the deal with Bill Lerda?"

Mrs. Hashim said tightly, "Sure I have."

Stroud shook his head. "I figured you had more sense than that, Fanny, and more love for your daughter. But all you ever did care anything about was them boys. They're gone now, though. And there's no sense in your sacrificing Cheryl's happiness just trying to get revenge."

"For years," Fanny Hashim said, "the Muleshoe depended on the law for backing and didn't get it. You didn't do a thing about Morgan getting shot in the back, and you haven't done anything about my sons. Now the Muleshoe will try something besides tin-badge law."

Stroud and Tolliver cut a quick glance at each other.

Tolliver said, "Keep your distance from a renegade bunch like that, and you're all right. Get mixed up with those Lerdas, and you'll never get loose from them."

"All you're fixing to do now, Fanny," Stroud told her, "is run through everything Morgan left you. But that's the way it usually happens. A man spends his lifetime building up something for his family. He dies or gets killed, and what happens? His widow scatters it right and left. Or goes crazy over some other man and lets him squander it."

"Except for Cheryl," Mrs. Hashim said, "my family is gone. I'll lose the Muleshoe, anyhow. So I'm going to pay Ben Gregory back for what he did to Morgan. And for what he did to my boys. I may never get another chance."

Tolliver shook his head. "You're hating the wrong man. Mark Connick bushwhacked your husband, and I'm pretty sure he had something to do with your boys being killed."

Mrs. Hashim put an intent gaze on him. "How do you know that? You weren't even here when Morgan was killed."

Tolliver only glanced at the sheriff.

"Morgan did have a falling out with Connick," Fanny Hashim said. "Over Cheryl."

"And Tolliver had a falling out with him over Lurelle," Stroud said dryly.

Tolliver glanced down at his boots.

"By rights, Fanny," the sheriff told her, "part of the Muleshoe is Cheryl's. You've got no call to throw it away, just seeking revenge on the Bar G. Take Cheryl herself. Why don't you come to your senses, woman?"

Fanny Hashim's features were bleak. "Bill Lerda is the fastest man with a gun I know, and the most dangerous, Jim. I've got no menfolks now to carry on my fight. All I have is Cheryl. I'm too old to get another man, at least one that's able to buck Ben Gregory. So Cheryl will have it to do. She owes it to Morgan. She owes it to her brothers."

Sheriff Stroud got to his feet, flushed with anger. He said, "I'm going, Tolliver. No use trying to reason with this fool woman."

"Don't try to law me about my daughter, Jim," Fanny called after him as he headed for the stairway. "Scott and the others will be back in a few days and you might catch hell."

Tolliver clasped his hands, elbowed his knees and said gently, "All that's wrong with you is just grief, ma'am. You figure you've lost everything worth living for. Other folks lose loved ones and bear up under it. You'll just have to play the hand that's been dealt to you as good as you can."

"Tolliver, I'm sick. Sick of this town and everyone in it. Just a bunch of gutless men and gossipy women."

"I know one of the women that's pretty gutless, too, ma'am, if you ask me," Tolliver said. He got up then and went downstairs, continuing on through the lobby. Sheriff Stroud was out on the veranda, still flush-faced.

"See how it is?"

Tolliver nodded, passing a glance over the public square, his attention settling on two men who stood in the shade of a live oak. Ben Gregory and Mark

Connick. Their head-to-head talk aroused Tolliver's resentment, and he thought: Ben's going to pay me what he owes me before he leaves town. Damned if he's going to beat me out of what's rightfully mine. Gregory and Connick were looking his way now.

"Let's go over and get a cup of coffee," Stroud said.

Tolliver stepped off the veranda with him, and then asked, "Did Morgan really leave part of the Muleshoe to Cheryl?"

"Wasn't any will."

They angled across the plaza, away from Gregory and Connick. Tolliver paid the pair no more mind. He said to the sheriff, "When is Bill Lerda taking over at the Muleshoe?"

"They're heading for the ranch tomorrow, Cheryl said. Her and Fanny. I reckon Bill will go along. Maybe Mawson, too. No Muleshoe hands in town. Fanny sent Phillips and Sturdivant back up there to see if they couldn't hold the outfit together till she decided on a ramrod."

Tolliver was silent until they were seated at the restaurant counter, and then he unpinned the star and pushed it along the counter to Stroud.

"Wear it, why don't you?" the sheriff suggested.

"I haven't got any business being your deputy. I'd just get you in trouble."

"What do you call trouble, man? Hell, I'm neck-deep in trouble now. And I was counting on you to help me out of it."

Tolliver put his attention on his coffee cup. "Well," he said finally, "if you had a warrant for Bill's arrest, I'd serve it for you. But under the circumstances, I don't see any way I can help you."

Stroud drank some of his coffee. "I know what I'd do," he said flatly, "if I was fast enough on the draw. I'd go over there and shoot him. You don't need no warrant for that."

"Why don't you go over there and have a talk with him? Tell him what's what. Order him to keep away from Cheryl. Warn him not to take that Muleshoe job."

"Me? I told you I don't aim to get myself killed."

Tolliver said, "If Bill knew how folks felt, and how much everybody thinks of Cheryl, he might listen. Those Lerdas don't want to foul their own nest."

Stroud was silent.

Tolliver finished his coffee, and said, "If you can't produce a warrant for him, all we can do is talk to him."

"Would you mind going over there and mentioning it to him?" Stroud asked.

"I don't feel like doing it from behind your star," Tolliver said. "I might try it man to man."

CHAPTER V

Leaving the restaurant alone, Tolliver looked around for Mark Connick, but the Circle C owner wasn't in sight. Ben Gregory was now in front of the saddlery. Tolliver crossed the dusty street and Gregory called to him, "Hold on a minute."

Tolliver stopped and waited.

Gregory approached him with a clenched fist, clutching a wad of money. Tolliver's mouth opened in surprise then, for he found something in Ben's features he'd never seen before. Ben Gregory was almost trembling with fear, his eyes holding a touch of panic.

"I've got over my mad spell, Tolliver, so I'll pay you what I owe you."

Deeply thoughtful, Tolliver said in friendly tone, "I wasn't worrying about it, Ben. I knew you'd pay me." He took the money, gave it a swift count and pocketed it.

Gregory started away, then stopped. "Don't guess

you'd want to help me with that daughter of mine, would you?"

"How, Ben?"

"Well, she's sort of taken a fancy to you, and you might talk her into coming back home." Gregory's gaze kept shifting.

"I'll see what I can do, Ben. I'm pretty sure she's ready to go home now."

Gregory lowered his eyes. A man drove a team of mules up to the water trough in the center of the square, harness jingling, and began working the handle of the pump. As if drawn by instinct, Tolliver turned to look toward Allenthorp's Mercantile. Lurelle was out on the store porch, and she waved a hand. Tolliver and Ben responded. After she had gone inside, Tolliver turned to Gregory. "Ben, I'll make a bargain with you. I'll talk Lurelle into coming home, and I won't ask her to marry me until I can take care of her as good as you do, but you've got to do something for me. You've got to keep Mark Connick hazed away from her. I don't want him messing around her."

"It's a deal."

"I doubt if I can trust you, Ben."

Eyes still fear-glazed, Gregory nodded vigorously. "You can."

"Then let's go have a drink on it."

They started off together, but when Tolliver headed for the Desert Star, Gregory stopped.

"I don't want to go over there."

"They serve good whisky, Ben. Besides, I've got to see Bill Lerda about something."

With harsh bitterness, Gregory said, "Running an errand for the old lady Hashim, huh?"

"What do you mean by that?"

"She made him foreman of the Muleshoe."

"But I'm not working for the Muleshoe."

Gregory essayed a smile of skepticism but produced only a grimace, and Tolliver thought, somewhat guiltily: He's scared to death of me. The rancher lowered his gaze to Tolliver's vest. "Where's that star?"

"I made Stroud take it back."

"When you hired out to the old lady?"

"Ben, I didn't hire out to her."

Gregory stood there, his thick-mustached mouth twisted. "I wasn't aiming to keep fighting her and Cheryl, now that those blood-thirsty sons of hers got their needings. But I reckon she feels like she's got to have my scalp."

"Let's go get that drink, Ben."

They walked on. A couple of Mexicans, Lerda watchdogs, dozed as usual on either side of the swinging doors.

A guitar, a mandolin, an Indian drum and a piano were going full tilt inside, providing rhythm for dancers. The girls were unusually pretty, but neither Bill nor Scott Lerda claimed one, considering all of them as too dangerous to mess with. The Lerdas' loot, much of it, found its way under the girls' garters, though, and all of them displayed expensive trinkets of silver and gold. Tolliver considered it a typical frontier-saloon gathering, consisting of cavalrymen, emigrants, freighters, buffalo hunters and renegades. But here the men moved more deliberately, and sought fresh air sooner when feeling themselves getting drunk.

Beyond the musicians' dais were two billiard tables, two monte tables and a faro layout—all deserted. Most of the gambling games in Eagle Bend took place in hotel rooms. Big poker sessions among the cattlemen, Tolliver had heard, were held in Sheriff Stroud's *sala*.

Stopping just inside the latticed half-doors, Gregory said, "I'll wait here till you tend to your business."

In the front of the room were tables, and a heavy mahogany bar ran along one wall. There were several vacant spots among the crowd at the bar, but all the tables were occupied. Old Jake Mawson sat alone at one of the tables, drinking mescal, and his seamed face bore a look of distasteful introspection. Rumor had it that Mawson, stove-up old cowhand that he was, supplied the Lerdas with tidbits of deviltry they never would have thought of themselves. Bill Lerda was yonder at the lower end of the bar, drinking with the barber from next door.

Tolliver stopped when the Bar G owner did, and said to Ben, "Keep an eye on old Mawson there."

He went into the room, loosening his Colt and thinking: I wonder if I can trust Ben? He would certainly need help from Ben with old Jake Mawson if Bill Lerda got rough.

Old Mawson didn't even glance up as Tolliver moved by the table, but he was aware of him, Tolliver felt. Knowing that Bill had hired out to Ben Gregory's enemy, old Jake was doubtless primed for trouble, seeing Ben and Tolliver together.

Beyond the billiard tables, the rear door stood open, and Lerda hangers-on moved in and out, but none seemed suspicious of him.

He drew a .44 cartridge from a belt loop and stopped walking, and the music ceased.

Lerda and the barber had their backs to him. He could see their reflections in the back-bar mirror, but Lerda's eyes were shaded by his hat brim. The renegade glanced sidewise then, and Tolliver saw his profile, his thick-lipped mouth and big-nostriled nose. The six guns jutting from his hips had ivory handles.

Tolliver had an overwhelming desire to check on Ben Gregory. But he would have come here anyway, without Ben, so what difference did it make? Tolliver thought: He wants me to talk Lurelle into going home, so I reckon I can count on him.

Tolliver tossed the cartridge.

It plunked onto the bar top near Lerda's shot glass and rolled in a circle, and Lerda came round like an uncoiled spring, the fingers of his right hand splayed.

The skinny barber backed away, mouth pursed, brows highly arched, and almost tripped himself in his haste to leave. His alarm quickly spread, and other customers left the saloon. The bartenders halted where they were, ready to duck.

"What's that for?" Lerda asked harshly.

"Consider it a warning. It's got your name on it. And the next time you scare Miss Hashim almost out of her mind, you'll get it. Through your brisket."

As boss of a tough gang of rustlers and accustomed to having local men defer to him, Lerda stared at Tolliver scornfully. "Are you a Muleshoe hand?" he demanded.

"No, but I've elected myself to stomp Miss Hashim's snakes."

"Who'd you ever stomp?"

Tolliver's tone sharpened. "I don't need any character witnesses. You heard what I said."

The pupils of Lerda's muddy eyes grew larger. His right hand suddenly dipped. Tolliver was waiting for that. He moved in fast, grabbed the gun and tossed it onto the bar, then slapped Lerda across the mouth. The thump of the weapon and the smack of the blow were the only noises in the room.

Head rocking back, Lerda scuttled away, his left hand hovering over his other gun. Tolliver had intended to hit him on the chin when he reached for his second Colt, but Lerda had unexpectedly crawfished. Edging around a billiard table, Lerda still hadn't reached for his left-hand weapon, and Tolliver thought, If he runs, I ought to jump on his back and ride him all over town. But Lerda had no intention of running. He came up with his left-hand gun and Tolliver slacked off on one knee, raising his own Colt. His shot blended with the renegade's.

Three fast explosions came from Lerda's gun, the slugs screaming over Tolliver; then Lerda pitched onto his face upon the green baize of the table, his head starting a billiard ball rolling.

Six-gun smoking, Tolliver glanced toward the batwings, and at that instant a bullet knocked him sidewise, the six-shooter in Ben Gregory's fist emitting a roar. Someone shouted with anger. More shots rang out, but Tolliver wasn't aware of them. His reeling senses were unable to fight through the curtain of darkness rushing toward him.

A mockingbird was warbling when Tolliver regained consciousness. It was perched atop a tree in Sheriff Stroud's patio. There was moonlight. Through the open bedroom doorway, Tolliver saw three people at one of the benches. The glow of a cigar informed him that one of them was probably Jim Stroud. They were out of earshot.

He had his pants on, but was barefooted and shirtless. His head ached. His brow was bandaged, and he figured he'd bled all over his shirt. Suddenly full memory returned and he reared up in bed, fighting a wave of nausea. Ben Gregory had shot him. Sorrow for Gregory filled Tolliver now. Ben had been scared to death of him and had taken advantage of his turned back.

Why? Not because of Lurelle. If he had married her and installed her in a *jacal* somewhere, he wouldn't have blamed Ben for shooting him, but as it was . . .

Tolliver swung his legs off the bed and stood up and shakily moved to the doorway. There on the bench in the moonlight were Jim and Felicia Stroud and Cheryl Hashim.

"What did you do with my boots?"

The sheriff whirled to face him. Felicia and Cheryl got up from the bench. The three came toward the room, and Tolliver stepped back to let them enter. Felicia lit the lamp. Tolliver noticed that now there was no panic in Cheryl's features, none of the wild fear he had observed in her before he put Bill Lerda face-down on the billiard table.

Felicia said, "This does not please me. Get on the bed."

"I'm all right, ma'am. Don't worry about me. If I can get up, I can stay up—like a buffalo."

"What do you think, Jaime?"

The lawman shrugged. "You know how cowhands

are, Felicia. Most of them haven't got a lick of sense."

"What time is it?" Tolliver asked.

"Near midnight."

"Lurelle gone to bed?"

In the strained silence, Tolliver glanced at them sharply.

Stroud said, "She lit out for home. You killed Ben."

Tolliver stiffened, his chin jerking up with shock. "I didn't shoot Ben. But Ben sure as hell shot me."

Stroud said dryly, "Didn't shoot Bill Lerda, either, eh?"

Tolliver sat on the bed, not listening. Gingerly he felt the bandage and tried to recall events in the Desert Star. He was positive he hadn't fired a shot toward the front of the saloon. Maybe one of Lerda's slugs had downed Ben. But Ben was still standing and apparently unscathed when Lerda's head bumped the billiard table.

"What investigating did you do over there, Stroud?"

"I got the facts."

"Like hell you did."

"You downed Bill and then you and Ben plugged each other. Wasn't that what happened?"

Tolliver shook his head. "Who told you that?"

"The bartenders. Everybody who saw it."

"Those bartenders didn't see anything. Old Jake Mawson—what did he say?"

"Nothing. The old man was drunk. I doubt if he

knew what was going on—or you wouldn't be here now. He would have bounced another slug off your noggin. You hit Ben right between the eyes, and that's right good shooting, Tolliver."

"At that distance, it's too good." Tolliver sat a moment in reflection, and then asked, "Who took Lurelle home?"

"Connick and a Circle C hand. They haven't been gone long." Stroud's squinted eyes studied him intently. "Be riding yonderly now, won't you? Out of the valley?"

Tolliver thought it over and glanced up to say, "You'd sure like for me to get real far now; wouldn't you?"

Stroud frowned at him in silence.

"Only place I'm going," Tolliver said, "is over to the hotel." He saw his clothing, freshly laundered and neatly folded, on a chair near the bed and began pulling on his socks.

Stroud tossed his cigar into the patio. "We won't have the ghost of a show when Scott and his crew get back from Dodge, Tolliver. It won't make a bit of difference to Scott that Bill had a chance to draw on you. But if you'll light a shuck out of here, maybe I can bluff my way through."

Tolliver's face hardened. He remembered then that Jim Stroud was a family man, and said, "I gave you the star back, Sheriff, because I was doubtful about Lerda—figured he would get in the way of a bullet. But you're not mixed up in it, except in your own mind. Go on like you've always done."

Stroud made a troubled gesture. "But the gang will try to peg out your hide. I can't just stand here."

"You asked me to talk to Bill, didn't you? So you tend to your own knitting and let me handle mine." Tolliver was still unable to grasp the full meaning of it: He had lost Lurelle. He muttered, "She thinks I killed Ben."

Stroud was listening closely. "Didn't you?"

"I believe old Mawson shot him."

"That doesn't add up, Tolliver. Mawson is a member of that gang—depended on Bill Lerda for grub and whisky. You shot Bill. Ben shot you. Mawson would feel more like patting Ben on the back than killing him."

"The old man might have thought I still worked for Ben. Seeing me down Lerda, maybe he thought Ben shot at him, too."

"Drunk as he was," Stroud said, "he could have thought anything."

Tolliver glanced at Felicia. "What did Lurelle say?"

"She was wild weeth grief."

"Felicia had to take a pistol away from her to keep her from shooting you," Stroud said. "Of course, Connick was egging her on," Stroud added.

Tolliver looked worried as he stood up. The womenfolk stepped out into the patio. Putting on his shirt, vest and gun, and carefully setting on his hat, Tolliver followed Cheryl and Felicia, saying to the sheriff's wife, "I'm much obliged to you, ma'am. From the way this thing feels, I'll have to come back and let you doctor it again."

"Thees is your home, Tolliver. Why not stay here?"

The sheriff said, "If you don't aim to leave the valley, you'd better stay here, so I can keep an eye on you."

Tolliver said, "Don't get in any deeper, Sheriff," and started out of the patio, feeling weaker now than when beginning to dress himself. He doubted if he could make it across the square to the hotel. Also, there was the possibility that one of the Lerda gang might be there to waylay him.

CHAPTER VI

At the passageway, he stopped, as Cheryl said, "Wait a minute, Tolliver," and she stood a moment longer, arguing with Felicia and Jim Stroud, as if they disapproved of her calling to him. Then she disappeared through a dark doorway beyond the lighted one Tolliver had come from. When she reappeared, she hurried toward him across the moonlit patio, slender and rounded and graceful, with a garment rolled up under an arm. Her nightgown, Tolliver figured.

"If you don't mind, I'll walk to the hotel with you."

"Just trying to give me a hand?"

"No."

Tolliver said, "If you had been aiming to go, Cheryl, you'd have been gone a long time ago. It's after midnight."

"I just made up my mind. I'm going back and stay with Mama. She needs me."

"Well," Tolliver said, "we'll have to take it slow,"

and he pushed away from the wall he'd leaned against.

The plaza was deserted, but the Brass Rail Saloon was ablaze with light and noisy with music. Across from it, the Desert Star was in darkness with closed doors—something that hadn't happened before, to Tolliver's recollection. It signified that the death of Bill Lerda meant a great deal to Eagle Bend's renegade element. Usually a saloon killing passed unobserved, except for drinks, set up by the house.

On the far side of the square, in front of the hotel, the eastbound stagecoach was just pulling out after changing teams, and its lights disappeared beyond Allenthorp's Mercantile, and the rig's passing left a smell of fresh dust floating in the warm night air.

Tolliver and Cheryl started across the west side of the square, moving slowly, with the lighted office of the Plaza Feed and Sale Stable ahead of them on their left.

"The way I understand it," the girl said, "you had a fuss with Bill Lerda over me and shot him. Then Ben Gregory took it up and shot you. And you killed Ben."

"I didn't shoot Ben."

"Who did?"

"I don't know yet. I haven't had time to try to find out."

"Mama said it practically gave the Muleshoe a new lease on life—shooting Ben Gregory."

"I'm glad somebody's happy about it," Tolliver said sourly, and presently told her, "Ben Gregory didn't kill your father, Cheryl. Mark Connick did it. He told me so himself."

Cheryl finally asked, in the same tone Stroud had used, "But why tell you? Wouldn't he want it kept secret?"

"You can make anyone believe a lie, Cheryl; it's the truth that people doubt and laugh about. Connick told me, because of Lurelle. I hurt his pride when I took her from him. But he's got to show me he's smarter than I am, and he'd rather brag to me about his deviltry than to anyone else."

"Trying to scare you, I suppose," Cheryl said. "Mark wanted to be friendly with me first, but Daddy wouldn't let him."

"Did you want to be friendly with Connick?"

"Oh, I like him all right," Cheryl said, "unless what you say about him is true. I sure wouldn't like a killer."

"That's what he is. It'll all come out, someday."

They walked on, Tolliver's thoughts still on Lurelle.

He had made a mistake in trusting Ben, there in the Desert Star, but he knew what Ben had been playing for.

Seeing what was going on, Ben had suddenly decided to kill Tolliver after Tolliver had shot Lerda, thus removing Bill as possible foreman of the Hashim ranch. Then he had taken a shot at Tolliver in an effort to wedge himself into Scott's good graces when Scott returned from Dodge, by pretending he had joined in the ruckus on the side of Scott's brother. That would have ended Ben's fear of the Lerda gang.

Ben had miscalculated, though. He had had a mortal enemy in the saloon, and whoever it was had grabbed his chance. I'm to blame, Tolliver thought. Ben wouldn't have gone there if I hadn't coaxed him.

"Sheriff Stroud said you'd gone to the Desert Star to talk to Bill Lerda, but I didn't dream you'd gone there to kill him."

"I didn't go over there to shoot him. He just wouldn't have it any other way. You have to *show* some men; they haven't got imagination enough to listen to reason."

"What did you all say to each other?"

"I told him to leave you alone; told him I'd elected myself to stomp your snakes."

Cheryl murmured, "I certainly need someone."

They had come to the hotel steps now, and Tolliver stood, summoning strength to climb them. The slug had glanced off the bone just over his left eye, and the wound throbbed acutely.

Shifting her rolled nightgown, Cheryl lifted his arm over her shoulders, saying, "Don't be afraid to lean on me."

Tolliver was blind dizzy when they reached the veranda.

The lobby was deserted, the old swamper busy with bucket and mop. The night clerk dozed at the desk, but awoke when Tolliver and the girl started up the stairway.

"Need some help?"

"No, thank you," Cheryl told him. "We'll make it."

She got Tolliver upstairs. She was barely able to support him by the time they reached his room, and he almost pulled her down on the bed with him.

"Sorry."

"That's all right."

He lay there for a time, breathing heavily, as Cheryl tried to ease his hat from under his bandaged head. Then she said, "I'll see if I can get your boots off." When that was accomplished, she asked, "Want your lamp lit?"

"It's light enough, Cheryl."

She glanced around. "But it'll be dark when I close the door."

"Don't close it. Pull a chair over here and put my six-shooter on it."

Tolliver was thinking that one of the Lerda gang might try to sneak in and knife him, not through loyalty to the dead renegade leader but with hopes of a reward from Scott. Old Jake Mawson, maybe. Sly old devil—Tolliver still believed that Mawson had killed Ben.

Cheryl got the chair and then asked with concern,

"Will you be all right alone? Want me to stay with you?"

"You get gone."

She stood silent in the gloom, then sat down beside him on the edge of his bed. "Am I worth two men's lives?"

"Not to me."

"Then why did you go over there and start a gun fight?"

Tolliver said, "Did your mother scare you into trying to find yourself a man before she picks one for you?"

"I was just trying to show you my appreciation. When I take a man for my own, he won't be you. That, I promise."

"Run along, little lady, and get some sleep. You've got more sense than I thought you had."

After she had gone, Tolliver debated about the door. Despite the risk of leaving it ajar, he decided that, feverish as he was, he couldn't get along without the circulation of air. He relaxed then, a blinding ache in his brow.

He didn't lie there long. A slight noise in the hallway tensed every nerve in him. He picked up his six-shooter and watched his door. He could see little of the hallway from the bed, but he knew someone was out there, approaching. He could hear a tinkle. Spur rowels on stealthy boots?

All at once then it occurred to him that maybe Mark Connick had only pretended to head for the Bar G with Lurelle. Maybe Connick was still in Eagle Bend, out there in the hall.

There was a scuffing noise. The tinkling stopped. The hall was silent.

Thumb on his six-gun hammer, Tolliver waited for the prowler to step into sight. But nobody appeared; the upper floor was silent. Tolliver's head wound was throbbing and his vision was hazy. Fearful that he would fall unconscious and be at the mercy of the prowler, he considered firing a shot to arouse the guests in the nearby rooms.

It wouldn't do any good.

The guests knew Tolliver. Some of them believed that he was tied in with the rustlers himself. The cattle buyer, Bigelow, had a room here, and might help him, but he didn't want anything further to do with that crook.

Eagle Bend folk probably figured that Tolliver's fight with Bill had been a falling out among thieves. They also believed, doubtless—since Sheriff Stroud did—that Tolliver had killed Ben Gregory, and such was the fear of Gregory's hard-case crew that no one would butt in if trouble started, feeling that the Bar G hands had a right to tally Tolliver. So now Tolliver was caught between the Lerdas on one side and the Bar G crew on the other.

He set his teeth against the throb in his skull and

pushed himself erect. Cautiously, he crossed the room in his sock-clad feet, gun ready, eyes on the hall. He saw no one. He eased into the hallway, and was startled.

He had expected to find someone standing erect. The man he now saw was seated cross-legged on the floor. It was old Mawson, battered hat pulled low, six-gun before him on the carpet.

"What are you doing here?" Tolliver demanded.

"Setting."

Tolliver lowered his gun. "I don't savvy you, old man."

"Well, the boys were talking like they might not wait for Scott, so I thought I ought to be here, just in case."

"Why are you siding me?" Tolliver asked. "I never did anything for you."

"Shooting Bill was right smart of a favor to me."

Tolliver studied him, eyes hard. "Is that why you kept Ben Gregory from shooting me again?"

"That's partly the reason."

"Then why didn't you tell Sheriff Stroud about it? Why let him believe I shot Ben? Anyhow, I don't want to be obligated to you."

"You'd rather Ben had let you have another slug, eh?"

Tolliver was silent, frowning.

Mawson said, "Rufe, you don't recollect very well, do you?"

"What are you talking about?"

"Me and you used to be right good friends, away back when you was a button. I rode for your pa in them days."

A distant look settled in Tolliver's eyes. With his boyhood memories came sadness. The cowhand he recalled had looked far different than this sorry, ancient scarecrow. He had been a prideful top hand, vain of his appearance. And he had gone by a different name. Tolliver leaned against the door casing.

"What's my old man's brand, Jake?"

"Circle Dot. Headquarters on the right bank of Ladino Creek, about a mile from the Colorado."

"I reckon you're him," Tolliver said reflectively. It seemed odd to him now that he could ever have known hero worship for the fellow hunkered on the floor in front of him. "How did you get mixed up with Bill and Scott Lerda?" he asked.

The oldster sat for a while in brooding silence.

"I don't reckon I've got any excuse." He drew a long breath, and added, "Wish now I hadn't done it, though."

"Why don't you keep away from that Lerda gang and work for me? I'm going to need hands pretty soon, when I get started running cattle on my place."

"Figure I can still make a hand at my age?"

"It would be worth trying. Are you telling me the truth—you didn't have anything personal against Ben?"

"Nothing against him."

"Well," Tolliver said, "you saved my hide, and I'll make it up to you, somehow. But I wish you had told Sheriff Stroud about taking part in that trouble. Lurelle Gregory thinks I killed her father, and I've been hoping to marry her."

Mawson said apologetically, "I didn't know that, boy. Reckon we could see her and talk to her? I'll tell her that you and Gregory came in there to clean out the Lerda gang and that her father mistook me for one of them. I had to shoot him to protect myself."

"I wouldn't want you to tell her anything like that."

"It won't make no difference what she thinks of me."

"It will, if you work for me. We'll have to get her to forgive both of us." Tolliver watched old Jake. "She won't be back in town for a month or two, possibly longer. Would you ride up to the Bar G with me, maybe tomorrow?"

"Sure thing."

"You don't need to guard my door. I don't sleep that sound."

"Go on to bed, boy. I ain't bothering you a bit, just setting here."

No trouble developed during the night, none that aroused Tolliver, and when he opened his eyes, it was broad daylight. He had a fever, he realized, and doubted that he could get out of bed at all on this day. He managed to do so, however, and glanced out his doorway. Mawson was gone.

A new thought occurred to him. If he took Jake up to the Bar G ranch, he would just be risking the old man's life. When Jake owned up to shooting Ben, the Bar G crew would be in a mood for retaliation. So would Lurelle, perhaps. Well, it was worth trying anyway, because otherwise Tolliver could forget all his plans of making the girl his wife.

After washing up, Tolliver lay back down, his head wound paining him, and he set his teeth against the misery. Outside, mustangs were whinnying and squealing in a nearby corral, and he heard the ring of the anvil as the blacksmith performed an early morning job—making hardware for Bill Lerda's casket, probably.

Spurred boots sounded in the hallway coming toward the rear, and Tolliver knew the steps were those of a woman. He had turned to watch the doorway when Fanny Hashim appeared, hat chin-strapped to her iron-gray head and weather-tanned features set in lines of satisfaction, almost of smugness.

"Still alive, Tolliver?"

"Of course. Come on in."

Fanny Hashim grinned. "I wanted to see if you were awake yet. Jim and Felicia told me to let them know when you woke up. Jim was here to see you, but you were sleeping."

"Tell Jim Stroud I said for him to keep away from here."

"All right. What do you want for breakfast?"

"Nothing."

Studying Tolliver's fever-bright eyes, Fanny Hashim said, "You're in pretty bad shape, and no doctor in this town."

"Felicia's a good doctor."

"She's good with bullet holes. And she's prouder of that badge Jim packs than he is himself."

Tolliver didn't feel much like talking.

Fanny said, "You must have beaten Bill to the draw."

"How'd you figure that out?"

"Cheer up, Tolliver. You may live it down."

She turned away abruptly then, going back up the hall.

An hour later she returned, bringing a tray containing a coffeepot and three mugs, a bowl of sugar, a can of milk and a square black bottle of liquor.

Mrs. Hashim put the tray on a chair, moved the lamp to the dresser and then placed the tray on the lamp table near the bed. She pulled the chair around and sat down, picking up the bottle of liquor.

"Nothing wrong with your innards, is there?"

"Nothing that whisky'll hurt."

Fanny uncorked the bottle and poured liquor into two of the mugs. Adding boiling-hot coffee, she tasted hers and added a little more whisky; tasted it again and smacked her lips.

"So old Big Ben Gregory double-crossed you, did he?"

"How do you mean?"

"Shot you, didn't he? Jim said Gregory talked you into tangling with Bill, and then he turned on you."

"Stroud will jump half a mile to a conclusion. Nobody talked me into it, unless it was you—the things you were planning to do."

"You eased my mind about my fight with Gregory," Fanny Hashim said, "but killing Bill Lerda made it worse than ever."

"Bill did it himself."

"Scott won't see it that way. He'll blame me and Cheryl for Bill's death as much as he'll hold it against you. He'll take his spite out on Cheryl."

Tolliver said, "He won't get a chance to, ma'am."

Mrs. Hashim lowered her eyes and sat for a moment with a frown on her brow. "Scott and that gang will be after your hide, but they'll want mine, too. With my boys gone, I need a foreman. Want the job?"

"I've got my own affairs to look after."

"Lurelle?"

"Yeah. Lurelle, and my place up in the Dragoon Hills."

"Lurelle will never forgive you for shooting Ben."

"I didn't shoot Ben."

"Maybe you can make Lurelle believe that, but I doubt it. Too many in that saloon say you did it."

"There wasn't too many in that saloon. They're just telling those stories to protect the old man—probably afraid of him."

"What old man?"

"Friend of mine. Don't be so nosy."

Fanny Hashim sipped her coffee. "I'll fix it up with Allenthorp's Mercantile and the bank so they'll honor your signature, and when you're able to ride, we'll pull out for the ranch. You can get on with the calf branding."

Tolliver picked up the liquor bottle and regarded it absently. "I wouldn't hire out to you now, Mrs. Hashim. Let's wait and see what Scott does to me about Bill."

She nodded. "Will you do me a favor?"

"If it's not a matter of life and death."

"Just keep an eye on Cheryl. I sort of lost her respect, and I don't think she aims to pay me much mind now."

"Don't worry about her."

"She's all I have," Fanny murmured, and sat there with her face falling into lines of despondency.

"Keep your mind off it, Mrs. Hashim. You've got a lot to live for yet. Your daughter will be getting married one day, and she may have a dozen kids. Then you'll start all over, making cowhands of your grandchildren."

Fanny's expression lightened. "That's true," she

said. "And from the way it looks now, they'll all be yellow-headed."

Tolliver stared at her absently, busy with his own thoughts.

Fanny Hashim finished her coffee. "Cheryl's crazy about kids. Fusses over Felicia's young ones all the time."

Tolliver rolled and lighted a cigarette.

"Ben's death is going to cause more trouble than ever," Fanny said suddenly.

"How?"

Fanny shrugged. "I don't know; I just have that feeling." She laid her hand against the coffeepot. "Want some more?"

"I'll take another dram of that whisky."

Fanny said, "It's all yours." She set the bottle on the table and stood up. "I'll take Cheryl some of this while it's still hot. And you think it over, Tolliver. When you shot Bill Lerda and Ben Gregory, you bought chips in my game, whether you were ready to play or not. So you might as well be on my payroll."

"Damn it, Fanny, I told you I didn't shoot Ben Gregory!"

Mrs. Hashim grinned at him. After a moment, she said, "We're two of a kind, Tolliver. You don't have to cover up with me. I know that Ben was gunning for you. He had to, because he couldn't keep Lurelle at home."

Tolliver waved for her to get on out.

CHAPTER VII

Tolliver took another pull at the bottle after Mrs. Hashim's spurs had receded along the hallway; then he stretched out on the bed for another couple of hours' sleep. He shaved and got into clean clothes when he awakened. Afterward he filled his belt loops with cartridges and looked to the loads in his six-gun, realizing he had to be ready for anything now.

Canting his hat carefully over the bandage, he went downstairs finally, intending to hunt up old Jake Mawson. If Jake would go along, as he had agreed last night, Tolliver planned to ride to the Bar G and try to convince Lurelle that he had not shot her father. But he wanted Lurelle to know that Ben had shot him. When she knew all the details, perhaps she wouldn't be too bitter, even toward old Jake.

Tolliver could not consider the possibility of losing Lurelle. That would be the end of his plans, and the end of the world, for all he cared. Now that he had fallen in love with her, he couldn't picture himself without her.

Entering the hotel lobby, he noticed a half-dozen guests in the room—army men, drummers, and a rancher from the lower valley, but his attention centered on Cheryl Hashim, seated on a sofa with the cattle buyer, Chet Bigelow.

That was a surprise. Tolliver hadn't known the two were acquainted. Watching them, he told himself grimly that Cheryl and Bigelow were even more than acquaintances. He could tell that from their faces. Tolliver scowled. Bigelow was no fit companion for Cheryl. As a matter of fact, he didn't place Bigelow much above Scott Lerda, since the man apparently dealt in rustled livestock.

Tolliver crossed to the sofa. Cheryl looked up, a pleased light in her eyes.

She said, "I went back to your room with Sheriff Stroud, but you were asleep. Did you good, too. How's your head?"

"My head's all right," Tolliver said impatiently. He put a hard gaze on Bigelow, who'd stood up, his thatch of cowlicked yellow hair as rumpled as ever.

"Are you and Chet acquainted, Tolliver?"

"Yes." Looking at the girl, Tolliver added, "Chet, huh?"

"Don't you think I'm old enough to call people by their first names?" she asked with mock haughtiness.

"That's not the point."

"What is the point?" Bigelow asked mildly, and because he was wearing a gun, he thrust both hands into his pockets.

"A while back," Tolliver said, "you tried to buy cattle from me. You implied I had some stolen cattle."

Bigelow shook his head.

"Maybe I'm mistaken."

Bigelow's mouth had a trace of a grin. "You're mistaken."

Tolliver decided not to push it further in front of Cheryl. Obviously Bigelow didn't want his shady cattle deals mentioned before her, and Bigelow had the appearance of a man able to take his own part if he decided to. But if they were on such intimate terms, why hadn't Bigelow protected Cheryl from Bill Lerda's advances? Afraid to buck Fanny's plans?

No, that wasn't it. Bigelow hadn't known of Bill's molesting her because, Tolliver decided, he would be the last man in the world to hear it from her lips if she loved him.

She loved him.

Bigelow's easygoing grin had deceived her as to his true nature, Tolliver told himself.

The cattle buyer stood there, blue eyes inscrutable, but he had taken his hands out of his pockets. Cheryl stood up, giving Tolliver a sullen glance. He said, "Stop hanging around this lobby alone, like a girl waiting to be picked up."

Bigelow said, "She wasn't all alone, fellow; she was with me," and then he turned to face the doorway as two men entered.

Both were lean-built, stern-eyed. Top hands, from the looks of them, wearing expensive hats and boots, and packing their guns in thonged-down holsters. In general appearance, years ago, Mawson had resembled them.

Bigelow said, "Well, howdy, Hutton. Made it, huh?"

"Yeah, we sure did, Chet. You busy?"

Bigelow grabbed up his hat. Cutting a narrow look at Tolliver, he said to the girl, "See you tonight, Cheryl. And don't do anything you don't want to do."

Silently, she watched him go out with the strangers.

Tolliver said then, "Stay away from him. You don't know anything about him. He might not be the kind of man you ought to be seen with. How long have you known him?"

"About a month."

"Well, he's no damned good. He handles rustled cattle—maybe even your mother's."

"I don't believe it!"

Her intensity surprised Tolliver, even though he considered her in love with the man. Strangely, he was angered. "If you're so high on Bigelow, why didn't you tell him about Bill? Didn't want him to know it? What *did* Lerda do to you?"

"Not enough for you to have killed him over."

They regarded each other resentfully. Tolliver said then, "Be careful who you get tangled up with. I might not be around next time."

"Chet's all right. You ask Mama if he isn't."

"I wouldn't take her word for it. In picking your men friends, her judgment isn't worth two whoops in hell."

"Mama was just worried sick and didn't know what to do. She almost died when she lost Lee and Cliff." She paused. "But you made Ben Gregory pay for it, didn't you?"

Tolliver gave her no answer. Presently he said, "Get on upstairs and stay with your mother, or go back over to Felicia's. You're not going to hang around this lobby alone."

Indignation flared in Cheryl's eyes; her mouth tightened, but she turned and started up the stairs, skirts raised.

Tolliver went out onto the veranda.

The cattle buyer was standing under a live oak over toward Allenthorp's Mercantile with a group of cowhands. Including the two who had entered the hotel looking for him, there were six of the newcomers with Bigelow. It was a tough-looking crew, and yet they didn't have the unkempt appearance generally marking brand blotters.

Tough crew at his back or not, Bigelow was going to get told off the next time Tolliver met him. Tolliver aimed for him to keep away from Cheryl.

He didn't feel too much like making a long ride, but his head would probably ache as much in his hotel room as on his horse, he decided, and went to look for the old man.

He found him in the Brass Rail Saloon, seated at a table and peering at a copy of the *Dodge City Times,* but Tolliver doubted he could read without glasses. Still, the oldster had sufficient vision for six-gun work, as he had proved with Gregory.

There were fifteen or so patrons in the Brass Rail, and Tolliver eyed them warily, unable to tell a Lerda man from anyone else. Taking a chair near Mawson, he said, "Wish I knew all your owlhoot pards by sight. I don't like to itch between the shoulders every time I turn my back."

"You ain't liable to have any trouble till Scott gets here."

"You don't think he'll listen to reason at all?"

The oldster shook his head.

"Will he hold Gregory's shooting against you, since it looked like Ben was taking Bill's side of it?"

"Nobody knows what happened, except you and me. But Scott's already on the rampage where I'm concerned. So I don't care."

"I sure want Lurelle to know the details."

The oldster sat for a time with lowered gaze, his expression one of brooding. Then, shaking off the mood suddenly, Jake said, "First let's get that off our minds, Rufe. Unless you feel like you ought to favor that wound for a few days."

"I won't feel any worse in the saddle, Jake."

Tolliver separated from Mawson outside the saloon, heading for the restaurant. Afterward, he went to the Stroud home, getting Felicia to change the bandage, and it was nearly noon when he and Jake took the road to the Bar G, carrying grub in their saddlebags to eat on the way.

When they neared the fork in the trail leading to Tolliver's place in the Dragoons, he found himself wishing that he and Jake were headed for there now to start work, instead of being on their way to the Gregory ranch. And he wished that Lurelle were up there waiting for him She wasn't, though, and at this moment Tolliver knew, as clearly as he'd ever known anything, that she would never be.

He rode on beside Mawson silently, and when darkness overtook them, they pitched camp on a flat near the river. After eating, they spread their saddle blankets and bedded down, using saddles for pillows. And long before daylight they were riding again.

The shake-roofed log ranch house was still in darkness when they came within sight of the Bar G, but the bunkhouse and the cookshack had lamps burning in them. Tolliver reined his roan off the trail to ride by the knoll where the ranch cemetery was. A mound of fresh earth lay there now, and Mawson said, "That's where they planted Gregory, eh?"

"Beside Lurelle's ma," Tolliver said.

"Well," Mawson said, "I don't regret shooting him."

"I wouldn't be here now if you hadn't," Tolliver said.

The jangle of the *cocinero's* triangle rang out, announcing breakfast, and Tolliver saw the outfit straggling toward the cookshack. Several of them stopped to stare at the riders skylined on the cemetery knoll. The hefty-built Kelse hurried toward the ranch house. He was still in there when Tolliver and Mawson reined in near the corral fence.

The air was filled with odors of hot biscuits and bacon and coffee, and Mawson sniffed hungrily. "Might as well put the feed bag on with them, hadn't we, boy?"

"The cook probably wouldn't feed us," Tolliver said. He was recalling the day he had quit here and had had to fight for a pinch of salt. Things might be different now, though, with Gregory dead. Kelse might not be so tight-fisted.

Only one Bar G hand was in sight, and he stood near the cookshack, watching Tolliver and Mawson with dour hostility. He was Garn Jepsen, rawboned and narrow-faced, with a scraggly brown beard and the pale eyes of a killer. Tolliver had watched Jepsen like a hawk.

It was the first time Mawson had ever laid eyes on Jepsen, but even at this distance he recognized a man on the prod. "I believe we've ridden into a hornet's nest, Rufe."

Tolliver said, "And I'm wondering if we're going to ride out again." He began to loosen his saddle cinches.

Jepsen called, "You've got a hell of a lot of nerve coming back up here, after shooting the boss!"

"Keep your shirt on, Jepsen."

Tolliver saw the foreman appear on the ranch house porch, and beside him stood Mark Connick. You could easily identify Connick's store suit, with his pants legs tucked into his boot tops.

"Stay here, Jake, till I find out if Lurelle's up yet." Tolliver went toward the ranch house.

"Connick, tell Lurelle I'd like to speak with her."

His narrow-mustached face wreathed in triumph, Connick said, "Speak with me. I do her talking now."

"Not with me, you don't."

The heavy-jawed Kelse was scowling. He said, "High-tail it, Tolliver, while you're all in one piece. Miss Lurelle's got it in for you."

"Let her tell me that."

Tolliver glanced toward the knoll where Ben had

been laid to rest. He might have come here too soon. He should have given Lurelle time to become accustomed to her loss. She probably didn't want to talk with anyone now.

Tolliver turned away, going back toward Mawson.

Spurs jangled behind him. He looked around at Mark Connick coming off the porch. Connick fell in beside him as he walked toward the corral. When they were out of earshot of Kelse, Connick said, "You're all through with Lurelle."

Tolliver came to a stop, squaring around.

"While you were up yonder at Ben's grave," Connick continued, "she wanted me and Kelse to shoot you with rifles. I'm giving it to you straight, Tolliver. She'll kill you herself if she gets the chance."

"She won't get the chance," Tolliver said, "and I don't figure you will, either. At least, not in the back, the way you killed Morgan."

"And his boys," Connick added.

"They weren't shot in the back, according to Stroud."

"They were shot, though." Connick grinned. "Got any idea why Ben tried to gun you in the Desert Star?"

"You had something to do with it."

"I told him you were laying for him. Told him you always sold your gun to the highest bidder, and Fanny Hashim had offered you a thousand dollars for his scalp. You know how he was about money. He believed it."

Tolliver said, "I ought to gut-shoot you, Connick."

Connick's mustached lip curled with contempt. "You're pretty stupid, Tolliver. You played right into my hands. You tallied Bill Lerda, and he was fixing to poke his nose into my business. You downed Ben, and that left the way clear for me to get Lurelle and this spread. The only reason I talked her out of shooting you is that you're still useful to me."

Beneath the hatbrim and bandage, Tolliver's features were pale with anger. He swallowed and asked, "How?"

Connick said, "Scott will be back pretty soon, and he's still a threat to my plans. I don't intend to walk softly every time I visit Eagle Bend, on account of him. Scott'll be after you because of Bill, and one of you'll go down. Maybe both. Of course, you could high-tail it yonderly, but you're too set on making a go of that squatter place Allenthorp foisted off on you."

Abruptly Tolliver swung around and walked on toward Mawson and the horses. Mawson said, "Are we leaving, Rufe?"

"Yeah."

Connick had followed Tolliver. Mawson turned to him, asking, "How about some breakfast, mister?"

Tolliver said, "Connick isn't boss here. You'll have to ask the foreman."

"Tolliver's not keeping up with the times, old man. I've been boss here for a couple of days. And you're welcome to go eat."

Primed for trouble, Kelse and Jepsen were approaching, and at this moment Lurelle herself appeared on the back porch. Wearing a gray skirt and a light-colored blouse, she was a sight to tug at Tolliver's heartstrings, but there was nothing sweet or sentimental in what she said.

"Kelse, don't you and Garn let that killer get away!"

Connick chuckled. "See what I told you?"

At that instant a six-gun roared. One of the men near the cookshack had decided to use the girl's anger as an excuse for a killing. Old Jake Mawson cried out and keeled over, then pushed to a sitting position. Tolliver was unable to help him because Kelse and Jepsen had charged forward.

They weren't fast enough. Tolliver whipped out his Colt. He buffaloed Kelse, slashing the Bar G foreman across the skull. Kelse dropped, temporarily stunned.

Lurelle screamed, "Get him, Garn!"

Tolliver shot Jepsen, accidentally hitting Jepsen's drawn six-gun and knocking the weapon from his hand. Jepsen scrambled to retrieve it.

At this instant Tolliver was knocked to his knees

by a blow from Kelse's fist. Before he could regain his feet, Jepsen was upon him, hitting at his face with the six-shooter, which snapped instead of firing as the man jerked the trigger. Tolliver tried to come erect again and fell back as Jepsen drove a boot into his belly. Lurelle cried, "Kick his face in, Garn!" but Tolliver caught a spur rowel and jerked Jepsen staggering. Jepsen went down. As Tolliver got to his feet, Kelse loomed over him. He hurtled forward and drove a fist into the foreman's mid-section. Kelse stumbled backward, breath whooshing out of him.

Jepsen sprang in and landed a blow with his gun barrel between Tolliver's shoulders. Tolliver's spine arched. He turned, hands groping for Jepsen. Tolliver got a two-handed grip on Jepsen's arm and gun. Kelse, however, had secured a hold on Tolliver's shirt and vest and hauled him backward.

Jerking free, Jepsen loaded swiftly and threw up his gun. "Step away from him, Kelse!"

Connick bawled, "Hold it! Don't shoot him!"

Jepsen stood there blinking. He and Kelse then sidled away, lungs pumping, and watched Connick puzzledly.

Tolliver walked over and picked up his Colt. He cocked it and watched all of them warily, fresh blood from the head wound staining the bandage. He set his hat gingerly on his head, then turned to the oldster.

CHAPTER VIII

Old Jake Mawson sat flat on the ground, holding his side, fingers wet with blood. Tolliver asked, "How bad is it, Jake?"

The old man said, "Keep an eye on them fellows, boy."

Several Bar G hands lounged around the cookshack, but Tolliver couldn't tell who had shot the old man.

Sprague, a wiry man with a spade beard, came forward. "It was aimed for you, Tolliver. The old man just stepped into it."

"Who did it?"

Sprague shook his head.

"Mark," Lurelle said to Connick beside her, "I don't understand you. Why did you make them stop?"

"We need Tolliver, honey. He'll get rid of Scott Lerda for us. He'll have to, to save his hide."

Jake said, "I hope Scott gets you first, Connick."

Lurelle looked at Tolliver. "He killed my father, and I want something done about it, right now."

"Ma'am," Mawson said, "Tolliver never shot your daddy. Me, I did. He was fixing to shoot me."

Lurelle studied old Jake, then asked, "How much did Tolliver pay you to say that?"

"Rufe ain't had money to buy anything. He's been skimping to fix up that hill place for housekeeping, and well you know it, ma'am. Not trying to run Rufe down, but I spend more in a week than he sees in a year. He didn't shoot your daddy, but your pa shot him, and I rode up here with him to tell you the plain truth about that saloon difficulty."

Connick was watching the oldster angrily and obviously wishing he could finish him off right where he sat. He might have, too, if Tolliver hadn't held the cocked six-shooter.

When Lurelle took her gaze off of Mawson, Tolliver, his gun still on the Bar G men, told her, "Have some of your men carry Jake over to the bunkhouse."

Lurelle shook her head vigorously. "Killer!"

Tolliver turned to Mawson's horse and tightened the cinches and brought the bay closer. Connick said, "Kelse, you and Garn help him load that old liar."

"Be easy with him," Tolliver ordered.

When Mawson was in the saddle, gripping the horn with one hand and holding his side with the other, Tolliver said to Connick, "Don't look for any gratitude."

"You'll be returning the favor before too long."

"Not where Scott Lerda is concerned, if I can help it."

Tolliver looked at Lurelle. "You're making a mistake, throwing in with Connick, because he'll take this ranch away from you. Acts like he's already done it."

"Mark." Lurelle turned to Connick. "Don't let that killer ride away with a whole skin."

"Don't let your feelings get in your way, Lurelle. Without Tolliver, I'll have to face Scott Lerda sooner or later. I'm none too sure I can do it and walk away."

Tolliver said, "Don't forget, Lurelle. Your father lived by the gun, and when you do that, you die by the gun."

"So will you!"

Mounting, Tolliver got the reins of Mawson's bay and led the horse out, wondering if he or old Jake would get shot out of the saddle. However, they started down the trail to Eagle Bend, with Tolliver doubtful if Jake could make it. Out of sight of the Bar G, Tolliver headed toward the Dragoon River.

With the early sun at their backs, Tolliver broke trail through the shadowy timber, avoiding deadfalls and arroyos. Presently he stopped in the shade of a cottonwood on a sand bar overlooking the main channel of the Dragoon.

"Let's see what that bullet hole looks like."

Pain stabbed him in the head as he sought to get the oldster from the saddle, but finally he got Jake stretched out on the sand, knowing he could never get him back on the horse without help.

"Blind leading the blind, eh, boy?"

"All we need is one eye apiece, Jake."

Tolliver took off his vest and shirt and put the vest back on. He washed the shirt and wrung it dry and tore it into strips. He cleansed the oldster's wound, finding that the slug had angled through Mawson's side. Binding the wound, he said, "Feel like it bored through your innards?"

"My belly's too empty to tell."

"That slug was meant for me, like Sprague said, but Connick wants to kill you now, for sure. He doesn't intend for you to say anything more to Lurelle about shooting Ben."

"She didn't believe me, nohow."

"You put doubt in her mind. She'll wonder about it, and she'll want more information when she thinks it over."

Tolliver stood then, gazing up the river. He could see nearly a mile of the channel, a rippling expanse of lead-colored water in the sunshine. Beyond the tall cottonwoods, in the far distance, rose the plateau, but Tolliver wasn't thinking of the caprock. His mind was still on Lurelle, her bitterness, the hatred contorting her pretty features. What hurt most was that she had thrown in with Connick. It might be impossible to win her back now, even if she did credit Mawson's story.

Whatever happened, Tolliver had to keep Jake alive, not only because the old fellow saved his life in the Desert Star, but so that they could try to win back Lurelle's confidence.

Observing Tolliver's remote look, Mawson said, "Don't worry, boy. You'll win that little gal back."

Tolliver said, "She's the woman I need—a fighter. Well, we've got to cross this river, and I don't know if it's swimming water along here. I'll try to locate a ford."

Tolliver put the roan into the river, but found the current too swift for safe crossing. He rode upstream and tried again. He tried the water four times without finding a ford. Then he hit some quicksand and rode back to the second bottom, circling the treacherous footing.

Breaking from the bushes, he heard a shout and saw three cowhands on the far bank. Two of them had ropes stretched from their saddle horns, pulling a steer from the river-bank mud. They must have been keeping the east bank under scrutiny; they had spotted Tolliver at once. They were Muleshoe hands; Tolliver knew them by sight, and called to Phillips, a chunky redhead, "It's Rufe Tolliver, Phil."

Apparently they hadn't heard of Ben's death. After a silence Phillips said, "Thought you'd quit working for the Bar G. What are you doing back up here?"

"I've got a man with me, back a piece, that's been shot. I want you to help me take him to your bunkhouse. I know it'll be all right with Mrs. Hashim."

"You seen her?"

"Yes. She wanted me to work for her."

The Muleshoe hands whispered, among themselves, and Phillips said suspiciously, "Why don't you bring him across?"

"See this bandage on my head?" Tolliver took off his hat. "I might get him halfway across, and drown both of us."

"Who is it?"

"Old Jake Mawson."

"Why, hell, we can't have him around the Muleshoe. He's Bill Lerda's right-hand man."

"Not now. Bill's dead," Tolliver said, and explained what had occurred from the time Ben Gregory had hailed him from the saddlery in Eagle Bend until Mawson had been loaded on the bay at the Bar G corral.

Phillips said then, his voice heavy with foreboding, "I hate to hear that. With Mark Connick bossing the Bar G, a man'll be risking his life every minute, riding for the Muleshoe." He paused. "What did you and Bill Lerda tangle over?"

"I was trying to give the sheriff a hand, and Bill pulled a gun on me. Ben Gregory wasn't taking Bill's part. He just thought he saw a chance to tally me.

Connick had fed him a bunch of lies about me and Mrs. Hashim."

Tolliver purposely did not mention Cheryl, didn't tell of Bill's molesting her. He felt no need of trying to justify the shooting.

The Muleshoe hands talked further among themselves, and Tolliver rolled and lighted a cigarette, waiting.

Finally Phillips called across the river. "We'll drag this critter out of the mud, then come over to get that fellow."

"Be obliged to you."

"You say Mrs. Hashim hired you?"

"The same as," Tolliver said, and then he asked, "Is this shallow enough here for a horse to wade across?"

"Not right here," Phillips said, "but we can ford it half a mile farther up."

Tolliver had never visited the Muleshoe headquarters. Later, when the five of them rode into sight of the ranch buildings, he saw that Morgan Hashim, like Ben Gregory, had built of logs and roofed his structures with hand-split shakes. The logs and the shakes were a weathered silver beneath the giant old live oaks which shaded them.

There were several corrals and a circular breaking pen, centered by a snubbing post and fenced by vertical poles. The main corral held a dozen mustangs, and Tolliver noticed a myriad of chickens and ducks. Some of the ducks looked like wild mallards.

One long barn gave evidence that the Muleshoe kept up horses and fed them for winter riding. A chuck wagon stood nearby, and Tolliver said to Phillips, "I figured you fellows were still out on calf roundup."

"When Mrs. Hashim and Cheryl left for town," Phillips said, "we came back in. Fanny didn't seem to know what she was going to do. She talked like she might sell this ranch, and none of the hands wanted to risk being shot at by those Bar G gunmen if Fanny aimed to let the Muleshoe go."

Tolliver nodded. "Still branding to do though?"

"Yeah. There's quite a few slick-ears left."

"Has Connick been stealing any of them?"

"I couldn't say, Tolliver. We haven't worked the range that far down yet."

"Mrs. Hashim doesn't intend to sell out. She wants a foreman. Why didn't she give you the job?"

"I wouldn't have it," Phillips said quickly. "Too much responsibility. I don't mind taking orders, and I'll even make a gun hand when necessary, but I don't want to give no orders. Might make a mistake and lose someone's life by it."

A Mexican youth was pedaling a grindstone, sharpening an ax under the blacksmith shed, Tolliver noticed when they rode in among the buildings. A skinny man with a young-looking face and white-haired temples was at the pump, filling the horse trough, and two young Mexican *vaqueros* hunkered by the blacksmith lean-to, *cigaritos* dangling from their lips. None looked like the sort to run from a fight.

The Mexican youth put down the ax and came to help with the horses, and the *cocinero* came out of the cookshack. He was Pres Warkenton, a lanky, leather-faced man with a steerhorn mustache. Drying his hands on his floursack apron, he looked at Jake. Even at that distance he could tell that the old man was hurt.

"What happened, Phil? Them fellows have a shoot-out?" Warkenton stared at the bandage under Tolliver's hat.

"Not with each other, Pres. Mawson got shot over at the Bar G, and Tolliver claims he got his in town."

Brushing his mustache, the cook said, "Bring Mawson over to the bunkhouse and I'll get my medicines," and then he turned back toward his own quarters.

They put Mawson on a bunk and stripped off his clothes. After Warkenton had donned his spectacles and examined the wound in Jake's side, Tolliver asked, "Mess up his innards?"

Warkenton shook his head. "He'd of been a goner by now, if it had. He's just lost some blood. He'll be lively in a day or two, after I stuff his gut with beefsteak."

The *cocinero* had brought in a cartridge box half-filled with bottles of medicines. He said, "I've got something right here for him." Uncorking a blue bottle, he fed Mawson two spoonfuls of it, and told him, "That'll knock you plumb out in a few minutes, old man." Putting his gaze on Tolliver's bandage, Warkenton asked then, "Want me to look at that?"

"If you don't mind, Pres."

Old Jake Mawson had passed out by the time Pres had finished with Tolliver. Then Phillips came down the room with a shirt he had dug out of his warbag. "See if this will fit you, Tolliver. From the looks of those shoulders, it may be a little snug."

Pres Warkenton gathered up his cartridge box. "Stick around, fellows. Bean time soon."

<hr />

CHAPTER IX

Mawson was still sleeping when lamps were
lighted in the bunkhouse. Phillips and three others
gathered around the table and started a pitch game,
while the rest stretched out on their bunks. Restless,
thoughts in a turmoil, Tolliver walked up to the
deserted ranch house and smoked a cigarette sitting
on the front steps. In one of the live oaks overhead
a screech owl cut loose suddenly, and he was re-
minded of the superstition that the owl was a har-
binger of death. Perhaps, though, the owl was tardy.
Death had already come to this Hashim family—in
a triple dose.

Listening to the muted night sounds, Tolliver pon-
dered his own predicament. What would be his best
move now?

Well, somehow he had to convince Lurelle that
the death of her father was planned by Mark Connick. Right now, that was the most important thing
in Rufe Tolliver's life.

Maybe he would have a better chance to straighten

things out with Lurelle if he didn't hang around this Muleshoe spread too long. He could head for Eagle Bend, load up with supplies and go up to his place in the Dragoon Hills and stay there until he'd seen Lurelle again.

But even as he considered it, Tolliver realized that his conscience demanded him to give Fanny Hashim a hand. He had to stay on here as foreman until Scott Lerda had been settled with, until Mark Connick had been put in his place.

Except for pulling bog along the river nearby, the Muleshoe hands were only killing time, waiting for Fanny to come home and pay them off. They didn't think they'd have a job much longer, so why sweat? Well, tomorrow he would change that, Tolliver told himself. He'd tail up the Muleshoe crew and start them working for the brand again.

Feeling easier in mind now, he got to his feet and went toward the bunkhouse. The four Muleshoe hands were still playing cards. Looking on for a moment, Tolliver said to Phillips, "We'll take the wagon out again tomorrow and get on with the calf branding."

The chunky redhead stared up at him, then exchanged looks with the other three players.

The young fellow with the white hair—Sturdivant —asked, "Where do you fit in here—Tolliver? Not long ago, you were ready to gun us all down—riding for Ben Gregory."

"That's right. But after I shot Bill Lerda in that Desert Star ruckus, Mrs. Hashim came to me and told me she figured Scott would hold Bill's death against her and Cheryl as much as he would blame me with it. She said we were sort of in the same fix, and asked me to be ramrod here."

"How come you all to be in the same fix? She have something to do with you shooting Bill?"

Tolliver nodded, and his eyes told Sturdivant not to ask any more questions.

Sturdivant said, "Well, that suits me. Be better if Fanny was here, though."

"I'll ride down to Eagle Bend and bring her home after we get a few irons heating."

Moving his gaze over the others, Tolliver saw that they were all of a mind with Sturdivant. Going out again, he headed for the cookshack. Lamplight shone from the room at the rear. Stopping at the open window, Tolliver saw Warkenton, seated on his bunk, pulling off his boots.

"Mrs. Hashim wants this outfit to get on with the calf roundup. You don't ever go out with the wagon, do you?"

"Gabino Montoya is roundup cook."

"You'll help him get the chuck wagon ready, won't you?"

Warkenton nodded. "With just me and the old man here, what if that damned Mark Connick makes a raid on us?"

"That'll be up to you. Can't you put up a fight?"

"I reckon so."

"Well, you'd better," Tolliver said. Leaving the old cook tugging dubiously at his mustache, Tolliver went to the bunkhouse and turned in for the night.

Old Jake Mawson was considerably better when he awakened, and ate the big breakfast Tolliver brought to him. Dragging a chair over near the oldster's cot, Tolliver explained his plans, saying then, "You'll be all right here. Warkenton will look after you till you're able to be up."

"Going to Eagle Bend?"

"When I get the roundup crew back to work."

"Wait three or four days and I'll go with you."

"You don't need to go. I'm not going to ramrod this outfit unless you ride for the Muleshoe, too. Let's stay here till we get ready to go up in the hills."

Mawson ate in silence.

"You're my ace in the hole now. Nobody else knows the truth about that shooting. And we've got to get Lurelle over her mad spell, or I'll forget I ever saw the Dragoons."

"Whatever you want, boy. But I've got a feeling I can't ever shake loose from Scott Lerda and his bunch. It's too late."

"It's never too late."

"You're young, Rufe. You haven't had many disappointments. Wait till you reach my age, then see how you look at it." Jake drank his coffee. "Don't head for town until I'm with you. I need to be along when you lock horns with Scott. Maybe I can make the rest of them keep out of it. Most of them will listen to me."

"The way you guarded the door of my hotel room," Tolliver said, "I'd say you didn't trust them very far."

"I was there just to show them I'd taken a stand. Nothing happened, did it? But they'll listen to Scott before they will me, of course," the oldster continued. "Anyway, I want to be around when you and him tangle."

Tolliver considered. "All right, then; I'll put off Eagle Bend until you're able to ride. From the looks of you, though, that won't be long."

Meanwhile Tolliver intended to work the lower sections of the Muleshoe range, bordering on the Bar G.

Hearing the Mexican youth bringing in the saddle horses, Tolliver carried his rolled bedding to the wagon, as the others had done. Warkenton and Montoya had the chuck wagon loaded, and a little later the outfit headed south, the chuck-wagon team traveling at a runaway pace, the *remudero* hazing the cavvy along behind it.

That night the Muleshoe hands slept on the ground, twenty miles downriver from the ranch headquarters.

With the rising of the morning star, they were aroused by the sound of Montoya's coffee grinder, and not long after daylight Tolliver was tolling them off on roundup circle. He made a hand by turning bunches of longhorns into the drive headed for the cutting grounds. From all directions cows and calves were converging now, and here and there lifted the bellow of an enraged bull. Dust rose everywhere.

The morning's gather was soon milling on the holding grounds. Riding over to Phillips, Tolliver said, "You and I had better do the cutting and roping. I don't know anything about this *remuda*. You come and show me a horse with a tender mouth."

They headed for the rope corral for a change of horses, and then found that Montoya had the noon meal ready.

After eating, Tolliver and Phillips rode into the herd of mixed stuff and began cutting out the cows with unbranded calves. They roped the calves and dragged them over to the branding fire. Here flankers threw the calves, and the Mexican *marcador* burned the Muleshoe iron on their left sides. A *capador* worked with the *marcado*, altering the bull calves with his knife. The *capador* earmarked all the calves and put the pieces of ears into his pocket to be tallied.

It was an inferno of heat and dust and smoke, with cattle bellowing constantly. The air was rank with

the odors of singed hair and fresh blood, but finally
the branding was finished, and the morning's drive
was turned back onto the range.

Tolliver unrolled his soogans, hearing the cows
still bawling in the darkness because of the strange
smell of their freshly branded calves. It was a pleas-
ant sound to a cowman. In view of Tolliver's suspicions concerning Connick's Circle C, the calf crop
here was larger than he'd looked for. There was no
sign of rustling. Mark Connick was after bigger game
than a few stolen calves.

The general run of Tolliver's thinking was glum.
For one thing, he doubted Warkenton's ability to
keep an eye on the Muleshoe headquarters. Tolliver
was afraid that Connick would manage somehow to
reach old Jake Mawson there in the bunkhouse and
kill him, to keep Jake from talking with Lurelle
again.

Connick's whole scheme hinged on his marrying
Lurelle and acquiring the Bar G. He had made
enemies of both the Hashim women, losing any
chance of winning Cheryl. Now, he would be finished
if he didn't marry Lurelle. He'd be finished for certain, Tolliver thought, if I could get him to pull a
gun on me. But Connick was too cunning to risk an
even shake. . . .

The next morning, breakfast over, the Muleshoe
outfit began breaking camp to move the chuck wagon
farther down the river. In gray dawn the horses were

caught and saddled and Montoya's team hooked up. The wrangler's rope corral was coiled and tossed into the wagon, and the *remuda* was again turned loose. Tolliver and the others loaded the bedrolls.

Walking over to Sturdivant and Phillips, Tolliver nodded toward the brightening east, at the silhouette of hills beyond the high red bluff of the valley's wall. "I'm going to ride up to my place today," he said. "I can just about make it up there and back in time to help with the branding."

Having learned Connick's scheme of stealing the whole valley, Tolliver was worried now about his own place. His buildings were ramshackle, but could be repaired more cheaply than new ones could be erected—if Connick hadn't taken his Circle C hands up there and burned those buildings.

Connick would gain little by such a move. Still, he would derive malicious pleasure from it, just as he had when boasting to Tolliver about bushwhacking Morgan Hashim, and about setting Ben Gregory after Tolliver's scalp.

The redheaded Phillips had rolled a cigarette. When he lighted it, he gazed at the bandage showing beneath Tolliver's hat. "Keep a sharp lookout crossing Bar G range," he warned.

The white-haired Sturdivant also glanced at the bandage. "Is that wound still bothering you, Tolliver?"

"It's doing all right, Troy," Tolliver told him.

Then he added thoughtfully, "If I don't make it back, keep the roundup going. Mrs. Hashim won't sell the Muleshoe. You fellows will have a job here just as long as you want one."

Phillips said, "Let Troy run things, Tolliver."

Tolliver gave Sturdivant a questioning look. The man nodded. "Go ahead, Tolliver. I'll keep everything going until you catch up with us again."

The other Muleshoe hands were in their saddles now and Montoya was on the spring seat of the chuck wagon, reins in hand. Sturdivant and Phillips mounted their own broncs. Sturdivant let out a yell that started the outfit down the river at the usual runaway pace, the cavvy lifting dust behind it.

Climbing astride his fidgeting roan, Tolliver rode east, through shadows still dense in the low places and thickets.

He followed the windings of an arroyo into the timbered river bottom and rode out onto the willow-green alluvial fan.

He put the roan carefully into the current and discovered that this was swimming water. Reining the horse back out onto the sand bar, he took off his gun belt and tied it to saddle strings. He removed his boots and socks and emptied the contents of his pockets into one of the boots. Afterward he loosened the cinches and jerked off the roan's bridle, securing it to the saddle horn.

Grasping the roan's mane with one hand and his

boots with the other, Tolliver again forced the animal into the current, and a few feet from the bank the horse was swimming, Tolliver alongside him, holding his boots above the water.

On the far bank Tolliver wrung the water out of his clothing as best he could and took time to dry his six-gun and carbine; then he rode on slowly, dragging his lariat so that it would dry, too.

He was on Bar G range now, not far from the Eagle Bend road. Longhorn cattle were scattered about and off yonder in the direction of the Bar G headquarters, many miles away, Tolliver saw a band of horses. Stopping to coil his rope, he kept looking toward the Bar G, the escarpments of the Llano Estacado plainly visible beyond it, and in the dim distance he noticed two moving specks that looked like men on horseback.

CHAPTER X

They were a couple of Bar G hands headed for town, probably. If so, they had either left the ranch long before daylight, or had pushed their mounts hard.

Riding on, Tolliver crossed the road, threaded among oak-covered knolls. Here the Muleshoe hands had warned Tolliver to keep a sharp lookout. But he himself was expecting no trouble from Connick just now; it was old Jake Mawson that Connick wanted. Tolliver told himself that there wouldn't have been any gunplay in the first place if Lurelle had kept her mouth shut. With her squalling for blood, there was small wonder that Mawson had got shot. Well, maybe Lurelle had cooled off by now and had taken a rational look at old Jake Mawson's words.

Maybe she had even forgiven Tolliver.

Nevertheless he found himself curious as to the identities of the riders he had spied off there to the north. He reined to the summit of a low hill, where he stopped the roan in the shade of an oak. Rolling a smoke, he scanned the terrain to the north again, closely.

He could see a long stretch of the Eagle Bend road, and now there were three riders yonder, instead of two. One was at least a mile ahead of the others, and was wearing something white, probably a blouse. Tolliver realized after a bit that the rider was Lurelle; the men behind her might be trailing her. Did she know it? She couldn't see them, because of the hollows and hogbacks of the road.

Tolliver longed to ride down to the Eagle Bend trail and wait there, to find out if Lurelle still hated him, and had the girl been alone he would have done so. Kelse and Jepsen could be the men trailing her, however, and Tolliver wanted no further trouble with them.

Putting the roan down off the hill, he reined a little more to the south and struck Laguna Creek. He followed its meanderings across the valley and into the canyon it had cut in the high red wall on the valley's east side. Soon the abrupt walls of the canyon gave way to cedar-dotted slopes as Tolliver went higher into the hills.

When the stream made a bend northward, he rode into a bowl containing about a section of level land, to which Allenthorp had given him a quitclaim deed. The man who'd squatted here originally had been killed by Comanches, and the Eagle Bend merchant had taken the place on a debt.

Within sight of his buildings now, Tolliver learned that he had worried needlessly. They hadn't been destroyed. Nothing was changed.

Laguna Creek here was a clear stream tumbling over rocks. The floor of the bowl was thickly carpeted with grass, and scattered about were boulders as high as a man on horseback.

Following the trail on into the bowl, Tolliver was riding north. Laguna Creek meandered along the base of the cedar-clad hills which hemmed in the claim on the southeast. A sizable barn, in fair condition, stood inside a corral on the creek bank to the right. Tolliver rode through the shade cast by the barn and continued on to the cabin atop a low elevation straight ahead, dismounting at the porch.

The house was really two cabins with a covered dog run between them. A rock chimney stood at either end. The porches were floored with thick puncheons, but the main house needed a new roof, new chinking and new window sash.

Pulling saddle and blanket and bridle off the roan, Tolliver used his lariat and staked the horse out to graze.

Afterward, as he always did when coming here, he spent a while just moseying through the house and barn, making plans, itemizing mentally the work to be done. He had even measured off space for a bunkhouse and had driven corner pegs. A well had been dug near the back porch. Tolliver planned to add a room which would enclose this well. He would install a pump, and the new room would be the kitchen. He had decided all this when making plans concerning Lurelle. Things looked different now, though. Maybe he wouldn't ever be able to bring Lurelle up here. As a matter of fact, his better judgment told him he wouldn't, but he kept hoping.

Without her he wouldn't have the heart to go ahead with his plans, and he didn't even want to make a ranch headquarters out of this place if Lurelle wasn't going to share it with him.

It all depended on old Jake Mawson, really—whether she believed the oldster's explanation of her father's death. Tolliver found himself worrying about Mawson's safety now. If Mark Connick decided to take the Bar G crew over to the Muleshoe to get Jake, there would be no one to stop him. Warkenton would put up a fight, of course, but one man couldn't hold off Gregory's hardcase outfit for long. If they wanted him, they would get Jake eventually. Perhaps, Tolliver told himself gloomily, he had done wrong in bringing all the hands off on roundup and leaving old Jake Mawson alone with the cook.

Squinting at the sun, Tolliver judged he had time to get in a couple of hours' work before starting back to the Muleshoe roundup. He got an ax and bucksaw from the barn lean-to and went out to the stand of timber east of the corral. He had already felled several trees and trimmed them. Lifting one of the logs onto his sawhorse, he began bucking it into bolts, preparing to split shakes with which to reroof the cabin, when he heard his horse nickering.

Tolliver walked up far enough to see the place where he had staked out the horse, and found that it was interested in something on the trail leading in from the valley. Making certain that his six-gun was fully loaded, he went toward the house, and came along the north fence of the corral just as Lurelle Gregory rode into sight from beyond the barn.

He didn't call out a greeting, nor did she. They met at the fence corner and stared at each other searchingly. Lurelle's features were grave. Tolliver was remembering how she had begged Garn Jepsen to kick his face in that morning at the Bar G, but now there was no fury in Lurelle's long-lashed dark eyes.

"Won't you get down?" he asked.

With the white blouse, Lurelle was wearing a gray riding skirt, and the hat slanted on her wavy hair was gray, too. Her saddle boot bore a carbine, and Tolliver also noticed a bulging pair of saddlebags. She let him help her off the white-stockinged bay mare, and glanced toward the cabin with an expression of deep concern.

"How is he, Rufe? That old man we shot. Isn't he in the house?" Her eyes widened with alarm. "Did he die?"

"Jake Mawson? I didn't bring him here, Lurelle. Took him to the Muleshoe. The cook patched him up and said he'd be all right in a couple of days."

Gathering up the bridle reins, Tolliver led Lurelle's horse closer to the cabin, the girl walking beside him.

He said, "I saw you coming down the road, but I figured you were headed for town."

"I was bringing some things I thought you'd need. Neither you nor the old man looked as if you could make it to Eagle Bend, but it never entered my head that you'd take him to the Muleshoe." She watched Tolliver ground-tie the mare and loosen the girth. "I heard you sawing something. Are you staying here and working?"

Tolliver shook his head and explained why he had left the Muleshoe roundup outfit.

Lurelle said then, "I don't see why Mark would want to destroy this place."

Tolliver looked straight into her eyes. "Knowing I wanted to marry you and move you up here would be reason enough for him. But now I can see that Connick wouldn't burn my buildings at all. Folks in Eagle Bend think that I'm tied in with that bunch of renegades and hide rustled cattle up here. Connick would want them to go on believing that."

"They don't think that, either," Lurelle protested.

"That cattle buyer, Bigelow, said he'd heard I had cattle, and I know he meant stolen cattle."

"Well, it's not true, so don't worry about it." She turned away and walked into the hallway.

Tolliver went over to his saddle on the end of the porch and got his carbine. He stood there for several seconds looking at the valley trail and listening intently. Tucking the rifle under an arm, he followed Lurelle.

She had turned into the cabin's west wing. There were two hide-bottomed chairs near the fireplace and in one corner stood a homemade bunk.

Tolliver took a drag on his cigarette. "You've changed, Lurelle. Toward me, I mean."

She shrugged. "I've been thinking about the old man sitting on the ground trying to hold back the blood with his fingers. No one in that shape would have said what he did. He was in terrible pain. And if he hadn't been honest, he would have been blaming you, not defending you. So I believe him. But what had Ben ever done to him?"

"Nothing. Jake shot your father because he was intending to kill me. Jake used to ride for us—for my father—and you couldn't expect him not to take my part."

Lurelle considered it with a hurt look in her eyes.

"Ben didn't like you, Rufe," she said finally, "but it's hard to believe he would try to kill you."

"Mark Connick had been lying to him and had him all worked up. Ben thought I was after him. He thought that Fanny Hashim was giving me a thousand dollars to tally him."

"Did Mark tell you that?"

Tolliver nodded. He tossed his cigarette into the fireplace and took one of the chairs, standing the butt of the carbine on the floor. Gingerly he pushed back his hat.

"You need a clean bandage," Lurelle told him. "I have some medicines and things in my saddlebags, if you'll bring them in."

Carrying his chair to the back porch, he brought her saddlebags and then drew a bucket of water. While she doctored his wound, he said, "Connick told me a lot more than that, Lurelle. Lots of folks thought your father bushwhacked Morgan Hashim. Connick did that. Sturdivant told me that Kelse and Jepsen and some of the other Bar G outfit killed Morgan's boys, but Connick told me he was behind that, too."

"Why?"

"Connick wants this whole upper valley, Lurelle. The Bar G and the Muleshoe, too. And if he can persuade you to marry him, he'll get what he wants. I couldn't stop him."

Lurelle said, "Mark might have told you that, just trying to trap you into doing something to get you into trouble, Rufe."

Tolliver made a gesture of resignation. "Go ahead and believe what you want to about him. I know him. He's a back-shooting killer."

Lurelle made no reply to that.

Finished with dressing his wound, she began putting her bandage material and medicines back into the saddlebags.

Tolliver carried her saddlebags back around to the front porch and after that he took Lurelle up to the stand of timber, discussing the repairs he planned and the changes he intended to make, and she seemed as much in accord with his plans as she had ever been. He hadn't lost her love even though he couldn't make her see through Connick's machinations.

He saddled his roan and rode back down the trail with Lurelle, and Tolliver kept a close watch for the pair he'd seen trailing the girl. He and Lurelle rode down into the valley without noticing evidence of anyone's being on her trail, and Tolliver decided he had been mistaken.

"I saw two riders quite a ways behind you this morning, and I thought they might be following you. Too far off for me to recognize. Know anything about them?"

Lurelle said, "It was probably a couple of the hands heading for Marshy Springs line camp."

Tolliver and the girl reached the Eagle Bend-Bar G road where they had to separate. There Tolliver stopped his roan in the shade of a live oak and hooked a leg around the saddle horn. He built a smoke and said, "What I told you about Mark Connick is true. But don't you start trying to check on it; no telling what Connick would do if you began bucking him.

Wish I could figure how to get rid of him for you. I don't like for him to hang around you."

"Mark's been a lot of help, Rufe. I owe him some consideration for giving Ben a decent burial."

Tolliver kept silent, not wanting to put her in a position of having to defend Connick. He also kept still about any plans of immediate marriage. She had inherited Ben's estate now, and until he had something to share with her, he didn't feel like coaxing her to become his wife.

Besides that, Lurelle was in no mood for such talk. She said, "You're taking the job as foreman of the Muleshoe."

"Just till Fanny Hashim can get someone else. Do you aim to keep fighting her?"

"That's up to Fanny. I certainly intend to hang onto what's mine, and if I have to keep on fighting the Muleshoe to do that, it's all right with me."

"Well, I can't blame you for feeling that way." Tolliver lifted his reins to ride on west. *"Adios,"* he told her.

Something in Lurelle's eyes caused him to rein his horse alongside hers. He leaned forward and took her into his arms and kissed her. She pressed her cheek to his jaw and murmured, "Be careful, Rufe."

"You do that yourself. You watch Mark Connick all the time."

CHAPTER XI

Calf roundup with no herd to hold was easier work for the Muleshoe outfit than next fall's beef roundup would be, for there was no night herding to do. Nevertheless, not knowing what Mark Connick might attempt, Tolliver had ordered the Muleshoe hands to saddle their night horses and stake them nearby when they unrolled their soogans. The Muleshoe riders had already swapped their saddles to their night horses and were eating supper when Tolliver topped out on the last ridge and spotted the wagon below him.

The cavvy was grazing half a mile to the right of the wagon. Tolliver rode in that direction and had the night wrangler rope him another mount. He swung astride the fresh horse and rode toward camp, approaching the fire from the downwind side.

Full dark had closed in, but Phillips, hunkered in the circle of cowhands, recognized him and called, "How did you make out, Tolliver?"

"No trouble. The place hadn't been bothered."

"Long ride for nothing, then," Phillips said.

"Well, I wouldn't hardly call it that." Tolliver was thinking that it was the most important ride he had made in his whole life, really, for now he no longer had to doubt Lurelle's love. It wasn't necessary to bring her and old Jake Mawson together again, either. She already believed the old man and hadn't seemed too bitter toward him. That was probably because Jake himself had been shot down right before her eyes. Also, she had seen Tolliver narrowly miss death at the hands of her own men and felt somewhat guilty, herself. Today's ride had taken a weight off Tolliver's mind and heart.

Getting a plate and cup, knife and fork, Tolliver helped himself from the skillets, Dutch ovens and coffeepot, then hunkered down between Phillips and Sturdivant.

"Did you see Fanny?" Phillips asked.

Tolliver glanced at him, surprised at the question.

"We met her this morning, headed for home. Her and Cheryl and some fellow I never saw before."

Tolliver had stopped eating. "Broad-shouldered man, kind of heavy built; yellow hair, blue eyes?"

"Yeah, he'll fit that. Do you know him?"

"His name is Bigelow. He's a cattle buyer. He's a—" Tolliver checked himself, not having any reason for cussing the man if Fanny Hashim had been with the pair.

Sturdivant said, "A cattle buyer? Maybe Fanny's selling the ranch to him."

"No. He was with them because he's taken a shine to Cheryl." Tolliver finished eating, got a second cup of coffee and rolled a cigarette. "Did Mrs. Hashim leave any word for me?"

"None in particular. She asked about the calf tally and wanted to know if Connick was stealing from us."

"He's got his sights set a lot higher than that," Tolliver said. "He wants the whole brand, not just a few calves."

"Fanny wanted to know if you were coming back," Sturdivant said, "and we told her about you and Mawson."

"What did she say about that?"

"She said there wasn't a handful of brains between you and Mawson both, riding up to the Bar G thataway, but all the same she was pretty doggoned pleased about it."

"Pleased about Mawson getting shot?"

"About you coming to the Muleshoe. She was worried about Jake and said she'd hurry home and see about him."

Tolliver finished his coffee. "You fellows keep on with the roundup, and tomorrow I'll ride up and talk with Mrs. Hashim. We haven't actually come to an understanding yet about the ramrod job."

It seemed only an hour or so later when Gabino Montoya's voice, saying, *"Esta amaneciendo"* to the day wrangler, awakened Tolliver. According to the Muleshoe roundup cook, it was coming morning. The moon was still bright and stars were gleaming overhead, but Montoya already had fresh coffee made and breakfast wasn't far off.

It took an hour to get the wagon ready for moving, to saddle up, and to take the kinks out of the half-broken horses ridden on morning circle. When this was done, Tolliver swung astride a deep-chested buckskin gelding and rode north, toward the faint, flat-topped scallops of the caprock.

Night had fallen again when he reached the lighted headquarters of the Muleshoe. Tolliver put his horse up and jingled his spurs toward the washbench. When he took hold of the pump handle, he heard Pres Warkenton, at the rear corner of the building, call, "That you, Tolliver?"

"Yeah."

The lanky *cocinero* came forward in the gloom, gripping a carbine. "Heard you coming and figured it might be you or one of the hands. But then I got to thinking that Connick might ride in noisy thataway, trying to fool me."

"Have you had any trouble?"

"It's been real quiet, Tolliver. And Mawson's doing fine."

Tolliver said, "Is that Bigelow around?"

"Uh-huh. He's up at the house with the women-folks. Well, Cheryl's old enough to be taking up with a man, anyway."

"She can do better than Bigelow," Tolliver said.

"I don't know. Except for them there fancy clothes," Warkenton said, "what's wrong with him?"

"I'll let you find it out for yourself."

Warkenton was silent, and then chuckled, saying, "You can use a bait of grub, can't you, Tolliver?"

"If you've got anything handy."

Following Warkenton into the cookshack, Tolliver watched him open the breech of the carbine to pluck the unfired cartridge from the ejector. Pushing the cartridge through the gate into the magazine, the cook placed the gun on pegs above his worktable and turned to the stove, fixing to build a fire.

"Ain't anything left but coffee, and it'll have to be warmed up. With the hands all gone, I haven't been doing much cooking. Just me and Mawson to eat. The big fellow eats up at the house with Fanny and Cheryl."

"Does he sleep there, too?"

"He slept in the bunkhouse last night. I've been sleeping there myself, so's I could keep an eye on the old man."

"Sleep in your own bed tonight, Pres," Tolliver said. "I'll be there with him."

The fire built, Warkenton got his personal towel and cake of hand soap and went out to wash; then he set about frying steak and making a batch of sourdough biscuits. Twenty minutes later he put a man-sized meal on the table, and when Tolliver got to his feet again he was feeling considerably better.

"How's that head? Want me to put on a new bandage?"

"Let's wait until tomorrow and put some court plaster on it," Tolliver told him, and headed for the bunkhouse.

Finding it in darkness, he lit the lamp over the card table and glanced at the bunk on which Mawson lay. The oldster was covering him with a six-gun, so he said, "Shoot, Luke, or give up your gun."

The oldster let the gun off cock and laid it on the chair beside his bunk. "I'm sure glad you're back, son. I've been in this here bed long enough. I'm able to fork a bronc. Let's you and me ride yonderly."

"Rest up awhile, Jake. You may not get another chance for a long time. When you get able to ride, I aim to put you to work."

The old man thought it over. "Let's try to talk to that little Gregory gal again, and then head back for town."

Tolliver crossed to Jake's bunk. "Everything's all right with Lurelle. She's still broken up over Ben, but I think she believes us. She's not bitter toward you, either."

"She won't want me around when you and her get hitched up, though. . . . Where did you see her?" Mawson asked.

Tolliver explained about his ride up into the hills.

Mawson said then, "Come morning, let's head for your place, Rufe, and get to work."

"Thought you wanted to go to Eagle Bend."

Jake frowned. "I don't care where we go, just so we leave. I don't like it here; I just don't feel welcome."

"You are welcome. Didn't Mrs. Hashim visit you?"

"Yeah, she was in. Her and the gal both. And that Bigelow."

"What have you got against Bigelow?"

"I don't like him."

"Well," Tolliver said, "that makes two of us, then."

Turning away, Tolliver went down the long room to a tarp-covered bunk that wasn't being used. Leaving the lamp burning over the table, he took off his hat and stretched out without removing gun belt, boots or clothing. He dozed off but didn't fall sound sleep. He awakened instantly, therefore, a couple of hours later at the scuff of boots and jingle of spurs.

Bigelow stepped into the room and halted, his high-peaked hat shoved back on his yellow hair.

When Tolliver swung his boots off the bunk to sit up, Bigelow had his gaze on Mawson.

Jake himself was paying the fancy-dressed cattleman no mind, but he had picked up his six gun and was toying with it, thumbing back the hammer, giving the gun the road-agent spin. Mawson flicked a look at Bigelow then, and an expression of killing hatred passed between them, or so it seemed to Tolliver. Jake was sort of underestimating things when he said he didn't like Bigelow, Tolliver thought.

The yellow-haired man was using the bunk straight in from the door, between Mawson's and the one taken by Tolliver, although there were other unoccupied bunks. Crossing the room to his cot, Bigelow cut a glance at Tolliver and said, "Howdy, snakestomper."

Tolliver began building a smoke, and he said slowly, "Well, Bigelow, she's got to have someone to look out for her. Father gone. Brothers dead. And I don't know anybody who can keep an eye on Cheryl any better than I can. You didn't do it. If you and her mean so much to each other, why didn't you do something about Bill Lerda?"

"You didn't give me time."

Tolliver considered it.

Bigelow unbuckled his cartridge belt and carelessly dropped his holstered six-shooter onto the floor. Sitting down to take off his boots, he said, "I didn't want to stick my nose into Fanny Hashim's affairs and make her sore at me. She'll be my mother-in-law one of these days."

"But you knew about it?"

Bigelow nodded.

"Did you notice how terrified Cheryl was?" Tolliver asked.

"I saw how scared she was, but she wouldn't have been scared if she had known what I knew."

"What are you trying to say? You mean that when the showdown came, you weren't going to let Bill have her?"

"That's it," Bigelow said. Standing up to strip to his underwear, he gave Tolliver a look of cynical amusement. "When you went over to the Desert Star and shot him, you surprised me. I thought you and him were *compañeros*."

"How come? You never did see me with him."

Bigelow turned, jabbing a finger toward old Jake Mawson.

Jake said, "I used to ride for his daddy."

Bigelow stood a moment with his lips parted, but said nothing. He put his boots under his bunk and arranged his clothes, placing his holstered gun within easy reach.

Tolliver moved to the door, tossing out his smoke. He turned back to Bigelow, saying, "How long do you think it's going to take you to wear out your welcome around here?"

"You own this ranch?"

"I've got an interest in it. Didn't Mrs. Hashim tell you?"

"She didn't say anything about you."

"Well, she should have told you I'm ramrod here."

"Those fellows with the roundup wagon were saying something like that, but I don't believe Fanny's made up her mind yet. Even if she has, it won't be hard to change."

"If I do work for her," Tolliver said, "men of your kind won't hang around here."

Bigelow stood there in his underwear, scowling, his gaze locked with Tolliver's cold stare, and then he padded up the room to the card table.

Perceiving the man's intentions, Tolliver said, "Don't blow that lamp out, Bigelow."

"It's bedtime, you damned hoot owl. I can't sleep with a lamp burning." He put his back to Tolliver and turned the wick down and blew the lamp out.

"What you need," Tolliver said roughly, "is to be taken down a notch."

In the darkened bunkhouse, Bigelow asked, "Why don't you see if you can hunt up somebody big enough to do it?"

"You wait till I talk with Mrs. Hashim and see where I stand."

"When you find out, come right on back and let me know, because I'll be waiting for you. Me and this old man."

"Boy, they ain't no use butting your head against a rock," the oldster said. "He's aiming to marry Miss Cheryl."

Tolliver said, "That's something I'm not any too sure about, either, Jake," and went on out.

CHAPTER XII

Outside, Tolliver found the night air warm and still. There was no moon, but the sky was full of stars, and the light from the ranch-house windows shone far out into the darkness.

Passing in front of the darkened cookshack, Tolliver heard the snorting of a bronc in the corral when all at once a racket sounded from inside the bunkhouse. Chair legs scraped and something made a clatter as though knocked over. Then the calm of the night was shattered by the explosion of a gun. Afterward come old Jake Mawson's voice, raised in angry protest.

Bigelow said, "Ah, shut up, you old devil."

Tolliver ran back inside the bunkhouse and lighted a lamp. When he looked toward Mawson's bunk, he saw that the cattle buyer, yellow hair tousled, had wrested the oldster's gun from him. Bigelow had picked up the overturned chair. He was standing there holding Mawson's six gun.

"Get dressed, Bigelow. They'll be coming to investigate."

Casting a startled glance toward the doorway, Bigelow turned and picked up his pants.

"Did he hurt you, Jake?"

"None to speak of, boy."

"Why didn't you shoot him?"

Bigelow said, "Why didn't he? He tried his best to."

"Before you got his gun, or after?" Tolliver asked.

Bigelow didn't answer that.

Tolliver glanced around the room to see where the slug had hit, and noticed a furrow gouged into one of the wall logs.

Mawson said, "I could have gut-shot him, if I'd wanted to."

"You should have done it," Tolliver said. "He was bought and paid for."

Bootsteps crunched hurriedly outside, approaching the bunkhouse. Steerhorn mustache bristling, carbine at the ready, the Muleshoe cook entered. Seeing that no one was hurt, he relaxed.

"Who fired that shot?"

Bigelow had pulled on his pants. He reached for the six gun he'd dropped onto his bunk and gestured with it. "I got tired of him pointing this at me."

Before Warkenton could comment, Cheryl's voice sounded. "Chet," she called, "what was that shooting?"

Moving in front of the doorway so she could see him, Bigelow said, "Nothing to worry about, Cheryl."

"It was an accident, Miss Cheryl," Warkenton said, stepping outside. "Everything's all right."

Tolliver went outside, too, and followed Warkenton as the cook approached the girl, and they met Mrs. Hashim, also.

She asked, "What is it, Presley?"

"Bigelow took the old man's gun away from him," the cook said. "They've calmed down now, ma'am."

"Do you think they have, Tolliver?"

"Yes, ma'am."

"Thank goodness, it wasn't another sneak shot from the Bar G. Come on, Cheryl; it's nothing that concerns us. You come with us, Tolliver; I want to talk with you."

A moment later Tolliver followed Mrs. Hashim and her daughter into the ranch house. Cheryl went on along the hallway without saying anything, but Fanny turned into the parlor and gestured at a horsehair sofa, saying, "Sit down, Tolliver, and tell me what was wrong down there."

This was Tolliver's first sight of the Hashims' living quarters, and he found the parlor floor richly carpeted, the log walls covered with plaster, on which hung framed portraits. On the mantelpiece stood wax flowers under glass. Several deep armchairs were placed about, and whatnot shelves containing bric-a-brac filled the corners of the room. The parlor was lighted by two porcelain-shaded lamps standing on the round marble-topped center table. On the table, also, lay a large gilt-edged Bible and beside it, an album of tintypes.

Tolliver said, "I can't tell you exactly what happened, Mrs. Hashim, because I wasn't in the bunkhouse. Bigelow said he got tired of Mawson pointing the gun at him. Jake is a little cantankerous, I reckon."

"Tired of staying in bed, I suppose." Mrs. Hashim settled down in an armchair. "Tell me what happened over at the Bar G when Mawson got shot."

Tolliver told her. When he finished, Mrs. Hashim said, "Do you mean to tell me that Jake was willing to risk his skin trying to convince Lurelle that you didn't shoot Ben?"

"Back on the Colorado River when I was a button, Mrs. Hashim, Jake was the top hand in our outfit, and I used to tag around after him. He took a liking to me, I reckon, and I believe he'd do anything I asked him to, within reason."

Mrs. Hashim thought it over and then she said with a grin, "Lurelle tried to get Connick to kill you, huh?"

"I didn't tell you all of it. I've seen Lurelle since then." He indicated his head. "She put this bandage on for me." He told of meeting Lurelle at his claim.

Fanny said, "That makes it all right between you and her, but all I can see ahead is more trouble if she lets Connick boss the Bar G." She sighed. "Am I going to have to keep fighting? Could Lurelle be silly enough to marry Mark?"

"She's got too much sense for that," Tolliver growled, "unless he forces her to, someway. No telling what he will try, because he wants to be a big rancher bad enough to kill those who stand in his way. I don't savvy him at all. He's got a nice little ranch down there, if you let him stay."

"If the whole thing would stop right where it is, I'd let him stay," Mrs. Hashim said.

After a moment Tolliver said, "Right now, I can't ask Lurelle to marry me, because I've still got Scott Lerda to settle with. And Mark Connick will have to be kicked off the Bar G to keep down trouble for you. But if I don't marry Lurelle, I won't have any authority to kick him off."

Mrs. Hashim said, "If it has to be, it has to be, and I believe in hitting first. When you get done with the calf branding, you could take our boys down the river and get rid of Connick's greasy-sack Circle C. Drive his men off and burn those buildings."

"I wouldn't do that at all," Tolliver said.

"Why not? His house used to be a Muleshoe line camp."

"That's what I heard, but Connick had your husband's permission to squat there. Not only that, Morgan backed him financially—and look what he did to Morgan in return."

"You're sticking by that."

Tolliver nodded. "Eagle Bend folks claim that your husband put Connick there to keep Ben Gregory from taking that part of the Muleshoe range."

Mrs. Hashim said nothing to that, and presently told him, "You've given me a new lease on life, Tolliver, and the hands, too. Phillips and Sturdivant and the rest of them seem like they were when Morgan and the boys were alive. No matter what's ahead, the Muleshoe will be a fighting outfit again."

Tolliver said, "I didn't do anything. The trouble was they just didn't know whether you were whipped or not."

"They understand now."

Tolliver built a cigarette. After a bit he asked, "Couldn't you find anyone besides Bigelow to come home with you?"

"You don't approve of him?"

Tolliver shook his head. "Should I?" he asked.

Mrs. Hashim said, "That's what I was going to ask you."

"You may be placing too much importance on what I think. But as far as fighting help goes, Bigelow's your man. You couldn't do any better in the way of a son-in-law than him. And he's probably got savvy enough to run any size ranch. But if he's the sort of man I think he is, he's not much above Bill Lerda. Could be that he's figuring like Connick.

Mark thinks he'll get the Bar G by marrying Lurelle. Maybe Bigelow has his eye on the Muleshoe."

Reflectively Mrs. Hashim said, "Cheryl was scared to death of Lerda, but I think she's in love with Bigelow."

She settled back and expelled a long breath. "I have reasons for paying attention to what you think, Tolliver. You beat Bill Lerda to the draw, and I didn't believe you could do it. You straightened things out with Lurelle about Ben's death, and I didn't think you could do that, either. I would have bet half I own on it. So it's whatever you say about Bigelow. If he's not the man for my daughter, then get rid of him. Run him off the ranch."

At this instant Cheryl cried, "You won't do any such thing!" Face flushed and deep brown eyes furious, she entered the parlor through an inner doorway, and said to her mother, "I'm sick of being talked about as if I were a prize heifer or something!" Whirling upon Tolliver, she said, "Chet is as good a man as you are. You just wait till——"

Cheryl broke off and turning, started to leave.

"Wait a minute," her mother ordered. "Let's thrash this out right now. Sit down, Cheryl."

Cheryl whirled back, chin high, and seated herself on the sofa near Tolliver. "What is there to thrash out?" she asked tightly.

"We have to decide who's boss around here—the man I picked or the one you've chosen."

"You've picked a hired hand, Fanny, and I've chosen a husband."

"Don't call me Fanny, or I'll get up and slap you right across the mouth."

Mother and daughter appraised each other in hard challenge. Then Fanny Hashim said, "Tolliver pulled me out of the most miserable predicament I've ever been in, in my whole life, Cheryl. He helped me get a grip on myself. And I'm still depending on him. You are, too. We're still in very grave danger from Scott Lerda and his bunch of renegades. I hope you realize that."

"I realize it, Mama, but we're not dependent on Tolliver. Not now. Chet will take care of us."

Mrs. Hashim said scornfully, "Yes, I'm sure he will."

Looking sidewise at Tolliver, Cheryl said to him, "You never have liked Chet."

"I never will like him, Cheryl. Or trust him."

Cheryl's pretty mouth hardened. "I don't guess you will, considering the type of men you ride around with. Didn't you bring that old renegade, Mawson, here?"

Tolliver nodded. "Yes, to keep him from dying."

"All the same," Cheryl said bitterly, "he's a killer."

"Hearsay, Cheryl. Can you name one man Jake has killed?"

The girl's lips parted, but she compressed them

again. Glancing at her mother, she lowered her gaze, hands clasped on her lap.

Tolliver got to his feet, giving Mrs. Hashim a level look. "I haven't changed my opinion of Bigelow any, ma'am. And if I'm going to be foreman here, I don't want him around."

"Then run him off, I told you."

Tolliver turned his gaze down to Cheryl, seeing only her eyelashes. He asked the girl's mother, "Is that an order?"

Mrs. Hashim said, "As far as I'm concerned, it is."

Still Cheryl said nothing.

Tolliver said good night then and went out onto the front porch. He stopped there for a moment, then jingled his spurs down the steps and around the house. He was about thirty feet beyond the back porch when he heard Fanny Hashim speak his name. She had come through the house to intercept him. He returned to the porch.

Mrs. Hashim said, "Tolliver, if you make Bigelow leave, Cheryl will go with him."

"We can't have that."

"Oh, no. She's all I have."

"If she really intends to marry him, Mrs. Hashim, I think it's all right."

Fanny Hashim was silent.

"Do you know anything about him?" Tolliver asked.

"No more than you do. Cheryl probably does, but she hasn't told me anything. But they really are in love."

After a moment Tolliver said, "You'll make it, all right, Mrs. Hashim. You've got an outfit of top hands. One of them can hold down the ramrod job if you'll give him a little encouragement. Ever consider Troy Sturdivant for that job?"

"I haven't considered anybody for that job but you, Tolliver. After Morgan was shot, I depended on my boys, and when they were killed, too, I just wanted to quit living myself."

"Well, give Sturdivant a chance, ma'am. With Cheryl feeling the way she does about Bigelow, I'm the one who'll be leaving. In the morning Mawson and I will pull out, if you'll lend us a pack horse and a couple of bedrolls."

"Take whatever you need," Mrs. Hashim said, and after a moment of silence, she added, "I hate for you to go, Tolliver, because I'm not at all sure about Bigelow."

"Cheryl seems to be."

"Yes. And that's why I'm so undecided. A woman's instinct usually tells her when the right man comes along. Cheryl says Chet is her man."

"Well, you can be sure of this, Mrs. Hashim: If she does marry him, he'll make her a good husband—or she'll make him a good widow. You have my word on that."

Mrs. Hashim said, "You and I are two of a kind, Tolliver. And as long as you're in this Dragoon valley, I won't worry a bit about anything. Yes, I will, too—I'll be worrying about you. Take good care of yourself, you hear?"

"I'll try to, ma'am," Tolliver told her, and he went on and entered the darkened bunkhouse.

Old Jake Mawson was snoring.

Bigelow said sarcastically, "Well, snake-stomper, did you find out where you stand?"

"Yeah, I sure did."

Bigelow laughed.

Tolliver stood in the darkness, fighting down his anger. Finally he asked, "What did you do with Mawson's gun?"

"It's there on your bunk."

Tolliver felt around until his fingers closed on the weapon. Afterward he said, "We're leaving here in the morning, Bigelow, and you'll have everything your own way."

CHAPTER XIII

During the night heavy clouds scudded across the heavens and rain spattered on the bunkhouse roof. Windstorms here reversed themselves in the summertime, and after a soaking downpour, the grass put out lush new growth that kept the longhorns fat all winter. Aroused by a thunderclap and a gust of rain-laden wind, Tolliver hurried down the room to shut the south windows, and Bigelow padded over to lower the windows on the east. Neither said anything, but both had the same thought: If this kept up, Tolliver would be unable to leave with Mawson come morning.

The rainfall was of short duration. Dawn was late, however, because the sky was still darkly overcast, calling for lamplight in the Muleshoe buildings long after the customary hour for daylight. Tolliver was reluctant to hit the trail in such threatening weather, but old Jake Mawson would brook no delay. Jake declared that he could climb into the saddle unassisted, and could stay there. He aimed to ride on alone if he had to. Tolliver offered no further argument. Under the circumstances, he was as eager to put the Mule-shoe behind him as the old man was. If Tolliver stayed here longer, he might tangle with Bigelow, and because of his regard for Cheryl, he wanted to avoid serious trouble with the yellow-haired man.

He and Mawson ate before dawn, and Warkenton inspected the oldster's wound, pronouncing the old man well enough to travel. Warkenton also looked at Tolliver's bullet gash and put court plaster on it in place of Lurelle's bandage.

After that, Tolliver rode to the meadow where one of the Muleshoe *manadas* was grazing. Leggy colts gamboled about, for most of the mares had foaled. Tolliver dabbed a loop on a mouse-colored filly with a back suitable for a crosstree packsaddle. He choked the filly down, took a half-hitch around her nose and after driving off the snorting, rearing stallion, he headed for the corral again at a high lope, leading his pack animal.

The Muleshoe *cocinero* was there to help Tolliver load up. Warkenton tucked in half a dozen cans of tomatoes before covering the grub sack and bedrolls with a tarp. He and Tolliver lashed the load on with a diamond hitch, then Tolliver went up to the ranch house to take leave of the Hashim women. If Bigelow was in the house, Tolliver saw nothing of him.

Old Jake had already mounted up when Tolliver returned. Cinches tightened all around, Tolliver entered the cookshack for a last cup of coffee. He told the cook, "If anything comes up and I'm needed, get word to me, will you?"

Warkenton took a swipe at his steerhorn mustache. "I savvy what you're driving at, Tolliver. Well, if Bigelow even looks cross-eyed, I'll bend a gun barrel over his skull."

"You might not know it."

"Don't you worry none about Fanny and Cheryl, young fellow. I'll watch out for them, and if it gets to where I can't do it, I'll call on the rest of the hands. You ain't the only one who ever threw a man-sized shadow on this range."

Tolliver's hard smile showed. "Well, I'll depend on you, Pres," he said, and started out.

"Good-by and good luck, if I don't see you again."

Tolliver halted and looked around. "That speech mean you're lighting out for other parts?"

"Me? No. But you'll be on the other side of the river, and there ain't never any visiting back and forth."

"If you're speaking about the Bar G headquarters, I don't figure I'll ever be putting in there. But my place is across the river, too," Tolliver told him, and went on out.

Riding south with old Jake Mawson and leading the well-loaded pack horse, Tolliver kept hoping that the weather would fair up, but the morning passed with no break in the overcast. In the middle of the afternoon a heavy mist started falling. The Muleshoe-Eagle Bend trail now ascended a long slope which led to a timbered ridge. Beyond the ridge was the spring where the Muleshoe chuck wagon had pitched camp a couple of nights ago. Drawing rein, Tolliver turned his horse to face old Jake Mawson. He gestured toward the *bosque* along the Dragoon. On the far side of the river lay the Bar G range, but they were miles below the Bar G headquarters.

Tolliver said, "Can you stand a ducking?"

"What for?"

"We've got to cross the river and it's deep along here. I didn't want to ford it back yonder where we might have run into the Bar G hands."

Hunched disconsolately in the saddle, the oldster said, "We can't go up to your place yet, son."

Tolliver dismounted, ground-hitching the deep-chested buckskin gelding he'd borrowed from the Muleshoe roundup cavvy. Drying his fingers, he rolled and lighted a cigarette. Looking up through sifting mist at the oldster's seamed face, he said, "We've got grub enough for four or five days, Jake. I counted on taking you up there and making you comfortable. Be easier on you. It's a long way to town."

Mawson regarded him without saying anything.

"Don't you aim to work for me?" Tolliver asked. "You said you were through messing around with that Lerda gang."

"Are you ready to move onto that place for good?"
Tolliver shook his head.

"Well, I reckon we'd better ride on down to Eagle
Bend, then, son. I'll go up in them hills with you and
make you a hand when you get ready to live there,
but I ain't going up there and stay by myself."

There was no use trying to change Jake's mind,
Tolliver realized. The buckskin was stamping and
switching, shaking its head to rattle the bit chains
and rubbing its tongue over the bit to rattle the roller
on the bridle bar.

Tolliver said, "Wish we had some slickers."

"We've got tarps," Mawson said, gesturing at the
pack horse. "And we ain't in no hurry. We can ride
on a ways and pitch camp. Almost time to cook and
eat, anyhow."

Tolliver gestured ahead. "Good place to camp on
yonder side of the ridge," he said, and got back into
his saddle.

They ascended the slope and went down onto the
flat, with Tolliver reining toward the spot recently
occupied by the Muleshoe chuck wagon near the willows below the spring.

Dismounting, he said, "This is about as good a
place as we'll find, Jake." Tethering the pack horse
to a sapling, Tolliver kept covertly watching Mawson
to see if Jake could dismount without causing himself pain. And when Jake swung down easily, he dis-
missed the oldster's wound from his mind.

Jake stretched to relieve the saddle kinks, and then he got his carbine from the boot. Tucking the gun under an arm, he said, "Build a fire and unpack, son, and I'll tend to the cooking," and he pushed through the willows in search of a place to wash his hands.

Gabino Montoya had left a few sticks of wood, Tolliver noticed, and the fire pit was fringed with charcoal. All of it was wet, but he whittled dry shavings and got a blaze started. He fanned the flame with his hat until some of the larger chunks caught, and then he piled on charcoal from Montoya's old fire. A few minutes later he had the gear off the horses, watered them and staked them out to graze. Cutting willow poles, he stretched a square of canvas to shelter their saddles and bedrolls and themselves, and by then old Jake had hot coffee and bacon and fried beans ready. The Muleshoe *cocinero* had loaned them a complete camping outfit, including a skillet and a granite coffeepot. Within a couple of hours, smoking and talking, Tolliver and Mawson had drained the coffeepot.

Mawson said, "Warkenton gave us a whole pound of coffee, already ground. I believe I'll make another pot."

"If you don't," Tolliver said, "I'll be forced to do it myself."

Chuckling silently, the oldster headed for the spring, coffeepot in one hand and carbine in the other. At that moment one of the tethered horses nickered a greeting to several broncs topping out on the hogback to the south.

Getting to his feet, Tolliver thought: It's Connick, for that was the direction of the Circle C. Still, the Muleshoe roundup wagon was down there somewhere, too. Maybe it was part of Fanny Hashim's outfit. There were six of them, all wearing high-peaked hats and yellow slickers. They were on the Eagle Bend—Muleshoe trail, which passed several hundred yards from Tolliver's camp, and they came on without slackening their jog-trot gait.

Down on the flat they left the trail, reining toward the campfire, and Tolliver recognized them.

It was the bunch of tough strangers Bigelow had been associating with in the settlement, the men whose appearance Tolliver had been unable to reconcile with that of riders who worked for a buyer of rustled cattle. Forty-dollar cowhands didn't ordinarily wear such expensive range garb or pack their guns in tied-down holsters, as these men did. If they weren't working for Bigelow, somehow they were in cahoots with him.

Picking up his carbine, Tolliver was standing beside the fire when the strangers reined in.

One of them said, "Howdy."

"Light down," Tolliver said.

He ignored the invitation. "Your name's Tolliver?"

"That's right."

"Mine's Hutton." Tolliver recalled the lean, stern-eyed *hombre* who'd spoken with Bigelow when Tolliver had told Cheryl to stop loafing around the hotel lobby as if waiting to be picked up. "How far is it to the Muleshoe?"

"At your gait," Tolliver said, "you'll get there about two in the morning. Light down and rest your saddles."

"We haven't got time for that," Hutton said.

"There's a spring yonder."

"These horses had water a little while ago," Hutton said. Carefully the newcomers inspected the camp, noticing the two saddles under the shelter and other signs which bespoke the presence of two men. The only place the second man could have concealed himself was in the willow thicket girding the spring; yet none of them seemed in the least curious about it. Having proffered a greeting upon riding up, the other five men were letting Hutton do all the talking.

Hutton now said, "You're the man who shot up the Desert Star Saloon, aren't you?"

Tone hardening, Tolliver said, "I don't recall ever shooting up the Desert Star."

"You killed Bill Lerda and Ben Gregory, didn't you?"

Tolliver considered it for a long moment before replying. "You don't look like the kind of man who'd run off at mouth unless you had some reason for it," he said slowly.

Hutton said easily, "I didn't stop by to pick a fight with you. Where are you headed?"

The velvet-like, well-oiled clatter of a Winchester action sounded as old Jake Mawson, screened in the willows, jacked a cartridge into the firing chamber. The mounted men shifted uneasily in their saddles. A couple of them looked gingerly toward the spring, but the old man was well hidden.

Tolliver didn't name his destination. He said, "The Muleshoe chuck wagon is down the river. You run onto it?"

Hutton said, "We came up the other side of the river. About four miles downstream, we met a man who said this side was Hashim range, so we crossed over."

"Mrs. Hashim is short-handed," Tolliver said, "if you're looking for jobs."

"You come from the Muleshoe?"

"That's right."

"You've got a place of your own around here somewhere, haven't you?"

Tolliver nodded. "A little place up in the Dragoons."

"Headed for there now?" Hutton asked.

"That any of your business?"

The mounted men kept staring at Tolliver through the mist, and one of those in the rear said, "Just don't bother about it, Hutton."

Appearing not to have heard him, Hutton asked, "Got any cattle up at your place?"

"Not yet."

"Somebody said you had a pretty good herd up there."

"Yeah, I know. Folks in Eagle Bend are saying that, but it isn't so. Bigelow asked me that same question, and I'll tell you fellows what I told him: If I did have any cattle up there and wanted to sell them, I wouldn't have to worry none about their brands. You can bet your bottom dollar on that."

"Is Bigelow at the Muleshoe?" Hutton asked.

"He was when we left there this morning."

Hutton picked up his bridle reins, saying, "That's who we're hunting right now." Then he glanced at those behind him. "Let's go, men."

They lifted their mounts to a gallop when they reached the trail again. Tolliver watched them over the ridge, and turned to cut a glance around at the thrashing willows where old Jake Mawson was emerging from the thicket.

"Took you a mighty long time to fill that coffee-pot."

"You didn't do no yelling for me to come out, I noticed."

"Why should I?"

"You wanted me where I was," Mawson said, "and you sure perked up a right smart when you heard me work this here carbine lever. Who were them fellows?"

"Bigelow's outfit."

Mawson said, "I should have knowed it. They acted just like him—low-down enough to rotten-egg a prayer meeting."

"Haven't you ever noticed them around Eagle Bend?"

"I might have. If I did, I never paid them any mind. Wonder what they wanted with Bigelow?"

"Well, now, you know as much about that as I do, Jake. Let's get some coffee made, huh?"

CHAPTER XIV

The mist disappeared and the sky began clearing as the day drew to a close. Mawson prepared supper. After eating, Tolliver got to his feet and picked up a club to use for a maul, saying, "I'll go move those picket pins before it gets dark, Jake, and give those broncs a bellyful of grass."

"Hold on, son. I've been doing some thinking."

"What about, Jake?"

Troubled, Mawson said, "I've got to be riding on."

"Thought you said we weren't in any hurry."

"Boy, I've got troubles I ain't never told you about."

Concerned, Tolliver frowned. "Well, tell me. Maybe I can help you."

"It ain't something you can help me with."

"You know what I think, Jake? Your trouble is mostly a craving for the bright lights of the Desert Star. You haven't had any whisky lately."

Mawson said testily, "That ain't it at all. And you

don't have to go if you don't want to. But I'm going to fork my bronc and get on toward town."

He began gathering up the utensils and eating tools. He scoured them with sand and then headed for the spring to rinse them. When he returned, he found that Tolliver had made no move to break camp. He picked up his bridle.

Tolliver said reluctantly, "Never mind, Jake. I'll go get the horses. But a man with a bullet hole in him oughtn't to push himself too hard unless he's got a reason."

"I've got a reason, son. We get to town, I aim to buy a stagecoach ticket and ride yonderly. It's not something that's just come up. I've been worrying about it for months."

"Are you ever coming back?"

"Sure. You offered me a job up there, didn't you?"

"That's why I asked you. I won't try to pry into your personal affairs, Jake," Tolliver told him.

Dropping his gaze, Mawson said, "Let's both of us high-tail it. You ain't got no business hanging around Eagle Bend now, not after killing Bill Lerda."

"If I ran, Scott would find me sooner or later. I've got to straighten it out with him."

Old Jake said wryly, "You will, boy, one way or another.'

Stars were glittering by the time they headed down the trail to the settlement. Jake grew taciturn, and Tolliver jogged along for hours, with only the thud of hoofs, the creak of saddle leather and the jingle of bit chains in his ears. Then Jake exclaimed, "Wait up, boy!"

Stopping the buckskin and the pack horse, Tolliver immediately heard the noise that had prompted the old man to rein in. Behind them sounded a steady rataplan of nearing hoofbeats.

"Come on, boy," Mawson said, "let's give him room."

"Why should we hide from him, whoever he is?"

"Come on here, Rufe!"

Tolliver turned his buckskin and followed Jake up a draw and around behind a brushy knoll that concealed them from the road. Dismounting, Tolliver walked back and watched the shadowed rider pass without slackening gait. One thing about him was obvious: if he was trailing them, he wasn't a very good tracker. Prints made by the saddle horses and unshod pack horse were plain in the wet ground, and the rider should have noticed where they had left the trail. Tolliver kept speculating about him, but Mawson didn't seem at all concerned with the man who'd passed them in the night.

"Who do you reckon that fellow was?" Tolliver asked.

"I don't have any idea, Rufe."

"Then why did you want to hide?"

"I've always shied away from strange riders after dark. Guess I'm just getting old and losing my nerve."

"Riding into the Bar G headquarters and telling them you'd shot Ben Gregory took plenty of guts. You had nothing to gain."

"Well, you would have done as much for me."

At daybreak Tolliver and the old man stopped for breakfast. When they had repacked and ridden on, they followed the tracks of the rider who'd passed them last night.

Tolliver said, "I figured maybe he was heading for the Muleshoe roundup wagon."

"He went on to town."

The south line of the Muleshoe range was just ahead, and they finally spotted Fanny Hashim's chuck wagon in the distance.

Tolliver said, "I was hoping it would be close to the trail, so I could swap this buckskin for my own roan. That's too far out of our way, though."

"Yeah," the oldster said, and presently he added, "Better take your mind off of Muleshoe affairs, Rufe. Bigelow's done cut you plumb out with that spread."

"He's done me a big favor. I've got enough worries."

"Ain't you a little bit late realizing that, boy?"

Soon Tolliver and the old man were skirting Circle C range. The enlarged Muleshoe line camp that was now the Circle C ranch house appeared deserted, Connick evidently having taken his crew up to the Bar G headquarters. Tolliver thought: Connick will stay there for good if something happens to me. As though championing Lurelle's interests, Connick would pick up the feud and go on fighting Fanny Hashim. Fanny, and her prospective son-in-law. Considering Connick's men, Tolliver ticked them off one by one. He could be wrong, but the Circle C outfit seemed made up of just average cowhands, not gun fighters, not back-shooting killers like their boss. So if Connick did stay on the Bar G, he would step into Ben Gregory's boots and let his own riders go. And Lurelle would probably be in accord with him. She hadn't really believed what Tolliver had told her about Connick. If so, Lurelle wouldn't have said, "Mark might have told you that just to trap you into doing something to get you into trouble." Tolliver was sure of one thing, however, concerning Lurelle. Thanks to old Jake Mawson's loyalty and guts, she had gotten over her mad spell. She still loved Tolliver. No matter what she and Connick had in common against the Muleshoe spread, Connick couldn't claim her for a wife. He won't, as long as I'm alive, Tolliver thought.

He and Mawson followed the river, the dense foliage of the *bosque* shading them from the heat of the morning sun, and they approached the town, which stood on the opposite bank.

Tolliver said, "Well, Jake, you got shot, but we accomplished what we set out to do."

"You've still got a mighty hard row to hoe, and don't you forget it, Rufe."

"What do you mean?"

"You figure you can talk your way out of a ruckus with Scott Lerda, but you can't do it. He's no hand for talking. Better come with me while you still can."

"You really intend to make that trip?"

"I've got to." Jake glanced around at the pack horse. "You know what I've been thinking? That filly is carrying a camping outfit. If I knew it would be all right with Fanny Hashim, I would borrow it and strike out horseback. Then I wouldn't be worrying about no stagecoach. When a man climbs into one of them things, he has to set there till it stops, whether he feels like it or not. On horseback, I could take my time if I wanted to, or hurry if I wanted to."

"Go ahead and take it, Jake. I'll square things with Fanny. But don't forget to come back. You'll be my foreman when I start running cattle under my own brand." He paused. "Don't light out without letting the sheriff's wife take a look at that bullet hole."

They rode on a ways, and old Jake Mawson said, "Let me give you some money to pay her for the filly."

"Fanny wouldn't take any pay if you intend to bring the horse back. Any idea how long you'll be gone?"

"Couple of weeks."

They forded the Dragoon half a mile above the Fort Concho–Fort Stanton stage crossing, and ap-

proached the Eagle Bend plaza along the west side
of Sheriff Jim Stroud's red-tile roofed *casa*. When
they reached the street in front of the sheriff's place,
Tolliver checked his horse. He got down to untie
the pack animal's lead rope, which he handed to
Mawson.

"I'm going to stop here and see the sheriff. No use
waiting for me. I'll catch up with you at the livery
stable. You won't need both those bedrolls, so we'll
overhaul that pack before you start out."

The oldster nodded.

Tolliver said, "In case I forget to tell you, give her
my regards."

"Give who—?" Mawson broke off and chuckled.
"Can't keep anything from you, can I? Yeah, I will.
I'll tell her all about you, boy."

"Are you married to her?"

"Not yet," the oldster said, watching Tolliver intently, and then he rode on along the street which
passed in front of the bakery-restaurant.

Two cowmen from the lower valley stood on the
restaurant porch, and Tolliver noticed several cowhands taking it easy between spring calf roundup and
fall beef gather near the water trough in the plaza's
center. The usual ranch rigs and tethered saddle
horses stood here and there. Army men, bull-whack-
ers, buffalo hunters and drifters thronged the fronts
of the business places along the side streets. Except
for a cursory glance, no one paid Mawson and the

pack animal any mind, because men were always
coming and going around here, with pack animals,
sometimes with a whole string, bell mare and all.
Nevertheless, Tolliver had a feeling that he and the
old man had been under hostile surveillance from
the moment they had ridden into sight of this town.

Well, that was nothing out of the ordinary. Members of the Lerda gang had watched Tolliver hostilely
since the day he'd shot Bill.

Leading his pack horse along the adobe fence, Tolliver tied it to the rack near Stroud's gate. The ornamental iron gate was closed. Approaching it, Tolliver found one of Stroud's diapered youngsters cling-
ing to the grille, peering out. Even as Tolliver
reached for the latch, Felicia came rushing along the
passageway. She snatched the child up in her arms
and scolded it in motherly fashion. Entering the yard,
Tolliver punched the youngster in the belly with his
forefinger and talked to it. He was fond of children,
but he also had savvy when it came to mothers, too,
and he wanted to please Felicia.

Looking at him with bright, dark eyes, she said,
"How did you make out weeth Lurelle?"

"We got her in a good humor," Tolliver said. He
walked with Felicia into the passageway where Sheriff
Stroud, cigar jutting from a mouth corner, was lounging in the doorway of the *sala*.

"Did Mawson convince her it wasn't you that shot
Ben?" the sheriff asked.

Tolliver nodded. "It wasn't easy, though, Sheriff. We had trouble with that Bar G outfit, and one of them shot Jake down, by mistake. He was trying to tally me."

"Jepsen?"

Tolliver said, "I don't know who it was." He looked at Felicia. "Mawson will be over here pretty soon to get you to doctor him up."

"Of course," Felicia murmured.

She moved away after a moment, going toward the patio where her other children were engaged in noisy play, and the sheriff invited Tolliver into the *sala*. Tolliver followed the lawman past the long table flanked with Windsor chairs, and sat down on the sofa near Stroud's desk. The sheriff dug out his cigars, and Tolliver took one. As he got it burning, Stroud brought out a bottle of whisky and two glasses. Pouring a couple of drams, he said, "Drink up. And any drinking you do from now on, you come over here and do it. I saw Otto Hahn over at the Desert Star yesterday. He was one of them helping Scott Lerda rail them longhorns to Dodge City. Scott may be back in town, too."

"I don't want to have to worry about Scott Lerda forever, Sheriff. If he's back in town, I'll see him and talk with him."

"The way you talked to Bill?"

"If I have to."

The paunchy, flat-faced badge-toter shook his head,

squinted eyes showing disapproval. "You won't get a chance to talk to Scott the way you talked to Bill—or the way they said you talked to Bill. Scott will move first."

"Well, when he does," Tolliver said, "you keep out of it." He picked up his whisky glass.

Stroud said, "Tell me what happened up at the Bar G."

Tolliver explained, telling the lawman of Connick's being at the Gregory ranch, of taking Mawson to the Muleshoe headquarters, and of Lurelle's coming up to his place in the Dragoon hills.

Stroud asked then, "Fanny act like Bigelow might be running the Muleshoe from now on?"

Tolliver nodded.

"If Cheryl marries Bigelow," Stroud said, "it'll be the best thing that ever happened to this valley. And to this town."

Tolliver said curtly, "You were right—your sympathies are all with the Hashims."

Stroud watched him steadily, a curious expression in his squinted eyes. He wanted to say something but was determined not to.

"Did somebody roust you out during the night?" Tolliver asked.

"How's that?"

Tolliver told about the rider passing him and Mawson on the trail.

Stroud said, "Whoever he was, he wasn't hunting

the law." Reaching for the bottle, Stroud refilled their glasses. "Did Bigelow follow you and old Mawson up to your place?"

"I didn't see any sign of him."

"Didn't hear what passed between them two, did you?"

"I just heard Bigelow tell Mawson to shut up. Jake should have shot him for grabbing the gun."

Stroud was silent.

Finishing his drink, Tolliver took a drag on the cigar and got to his feet.

"Remember what I told you," Stroud said. "Keep your eye peeled."

"Remember what I told you, too, Sheriff. Keep out of it. I don't need your help and don't want it."

"You'll need someone's help."

Tolliver said, "Well, now, maybe not, Sheriff," and went out to his horse.

He rode on to the livery stable and took the buckskin into the corral. Several cowhands were about, but old Jake Mawson wasn't, and the packsaddle had already been stripped off the Muleshoe filly.

Tolliver found his attention fixed on a different horse then, a dun gelding, a familiar one. He moved around to look at the dun's brand and found the Bar G iron stamped on its hip. Turning to the bearded hostler when the fellow appeared from the stable office, Tolliver asked, "How long has this horse been here?"

"Came in last night, Tolliver."

"Who was riding it?"

"I'll have to look at the book."

"Wasn't Lurelle, was it?"

"No," the stableman said. "If it had been her, the night man would have mentioned it."

Tolliver followed the hostler into the office through the side door, learned that the gelding had been stabled here by Walt Sprague. Taking his carbine, he angled across the plaza toward the big adobe building which contained the stage station, express office and hotel. He wasn't sure, of course, that Sprague had been the rider who'd passed him and Mawson in the night, but it could have been Sprague. The Bar G–Eagle Bend trail being on the east side of the Dragoon all the way down the valley, anyone coming from that ranch would not need to cross over and use the Muleshoe trail. If Sprague had done that, it could be he had been to the Muleshoe in search of Tolliver and had learned that Tolliver was on the trail to town.

Tolliver frowned. Letting Jake talk him into riding up the draw had been a mistake, maybe.

Worried, Tolliver entered the lobby, cast a glance over those seated about the room, and turned to the desk.

"Is Walt Sprague here?" he asked.

The fat-faced clerk said, "He's up in your room, Tolliver, so as not to miss you when you showed up."

"I'll see what he wants," Tolliver said, and jingled his spurs up to the second floor, turning toward his quarters in the rear of the building.

His door was shut but not barred, and he entered the room without arousing the wiry, spade-bearded man on the bed. Taking his carbine by the barrel, Tolliver dropped the butt of it noisily to the floor, and Sprague opened his eyes. At sight of Tolliver, he became fully awake. He sat up.

"Lurelle sent me to find you, Tolliver. She said tell you that you was right about her being followed, and Connick won't let her leave the ranch now. She wants you to come and get her."

Tolliver said, "Why didn't you bring her with you, Sprague?"

Features twisting into a grimace, Sprague said, "Man, you know I'm not a match for Mark Connick."

"None of the Bar G crew would side you, huh?"

Sprague shook his head. "They're still taking orders from Kelse, and he won't pay any attention to what Lurelle says. Connick's got him eating out of his hand."

"How about Connick's crew? Some of them were there the other day."

"They all rattled their hocks not long after you and the old man left. Didn't Lurelle tell you? They didn't like it when Gil Dobbs shot the old man down."

"Dobbs, huh? You said he was trying to tally me."

Sprague said, "That's the way it looked," and reached for his boots. He pulled them on and stood up to buckle his gun belt around him and to set on his hat.

"Did you meet Bigelow's men on the trail?" Tolliver asked.

"Six of them? Wearing slickers?"

Tolliver nodded.

"I didn't meet them. I rode around them, thinking they were Muleshoe hands."

"You didn't have any trouble at the Muleshoe headquarters, did you?"

"No. I didn't see anyone but Warkenton."

Tolliver stood his carbine against the wall and took off his hat. "Lurelle's not in any personal danger up there. Connick couldn't afford to hurt her."

"He'll try to make her marry him."

"He'll have to come to town with her to do that, Sprague, and Connick's not ready to make that kind of a play. I'm going to shave and clean up, and while I'm doing that, you go and get something to eat. Save time. And I'll meet you at the sheriff's office."

"Jim Stroud won't do anything."

"He'll deputize us. I aim to get shut of those gunmen up there and do it legally."

CHAPTER XV

When Tolliver came back downstairs, he found the lobby deserted. Observing, too, that the clerk was no longer at the desk, he slowed his stride, brows knitted. He continued on the veranda, carbine under an arm, and stood there moving a searching gaze over the plaza and the buildings which flanked it.

Fewer men were in sight now, and those who were seemed no longer lounging at ease. Most of them had their faces toward the hotel, as though watching Tolliver. Some of the rigs had been moved off the square, Tolliver noticed, and so had several of the saddle horses. Getting them out of the way of stray slugs, maybe. As Stroud had warned him, it was the Lerda gang. Scott was back and the renegades were up to something. Tolliver was almost positive of this, for the workaday noises of Eagle Bend had stilled, as if the townsfolk were waiting for something, and only the gang of *ladrones* who held Eagle Bend citizens in mortal fear could quiet down the town in a matter of minutes.

Tolliver's attention fastened on the Desert Star, upon the men occupying its porch. One had his hat in his hands. Tolliver started down the steps of the hotel veranda, and the man on the saloon porch put his hat on—and took it off again. He was signaling somebody, Tolliver thought, and started across the street, the Fort Concho–Fort Stanton stage road already becoming dusty again after yesterday's rain.

Tolliver had been expecting trouble. He wasn't afraid of a bushwhack bullet from the brother of the man he'd shot it out with, but he knew now it was futile to think of reasoning with Scott Lerda. He had to fight Scott, and it wasn't going to be long in coming.

Tolliver thought his trouble would come from the direction of the Desert Star, but he was wrong about this, too. Behind him, he heard a rataplan of hoof-beats. Whirling around, he saw several riders bearing down upon him, coming from either end of the big adobe hotel building.

Raising the carbine with hammer thumbed back, Tolliver squeezed the trigger and the gun exploded, but in the last brief instant he spoiled his own aim, unable to empty a saddle, unwilling to shoot a man not holding a gun.

There were eight of them, rough-looking, vicious-eyed, but intent upon roping and tying Tolliver, not killing him. They were twirling lariats, and except for the roar of Tolliver's carbine, the thud of their horses' hoofs and the swishing of the ropes, they overwhelmed Tolliver silently. The loops knocked his hat off and pulled the carbine from his hands. They jerked him down. Grasping a taut rope, he got up, feeling for his six gun. With a deft flip of the wrist, one of the renegades sent a hitch curling down his rope to slap the Colt from Tolliver's fingers, lifting a stinging welt across the back of his hand. He went down again, and a man yelled, "Give it to him, Lonnie!"

The renegade named Lonnie spurred his horse close. He swung down from the saddle, drew his six gun and swung a hard blow at Tolliver's head, and Tolliver's senses left him.

Vaguely he heard a coarse voice say, "Right there, Purkey," and then the shock of hitting hard ground after sliding headlong from the saddle he'd been draped across brought him back to full consciousness. A quick glance at his surroundings revealed that he hadn't traveled far; he was in front of the *jacal* behind the Desert Star Saloon.

No one was in sight around any of the huts, not even the Mexican girls who hung out there usually, but Tolliver was sure Scott Lerda was somewhere about. It flashed through Tolliver's mind then that old Jake Mawson, in some manner, either at the Bar G or at the Muleshoe, had learned of Scott Lerda's return to Eagle Bend. Jake's "trip" was really inspired by fear of Bill's brother, and not by a desire to visit a woman. The oldster was planning to get gone for good. Where was he now? Hiding out, probably.

Tolliver stood up, surrounded by mounted men, except for the renegade who'd dismounted to hold him under gun point, and he stood there, dusty and disheveled, the hot sun beating down on his tousled head. He looked toward the rear of the saloon as the others were doing.

Music continued to emanate from the Desert Star, along with other sounds of revelry—doubtless at the order of Scott Lerda. None of the customers had rushed outside to watch the men in the alley, probably for the same reason. Only Scott Lerda himself appeared.

He lacked several years of being as old as the Lerda whom Tolliver had shot it out with there in the saloon, but he had the same heavy-set build as Bill, and the same thick lips and Mongoloid nose. He was a brown-haired man in need of a haircut and shave and wearing a misshapen black hat, grease-slick black pants, a dirty flannel shirt, a soiled neckerchief and an unbuttoned vest with a torn lining. Tolliver observed, also, that Lerda's run-over boots bore spurs with large, cruelly sharp rowels and that the renegade packed two tied-down guns.

Scott put his attention on Lonnie Antrim.

Short and skinny of build, pinched of feature and

pale blond, Antrim was the youngest member of the Lerda gang and Tolliver now recalled something old Jake had told him. Antrim was the fastest hand with a six gun he had ever seen, and that was saying plenty, considering the gun-throwers the oldster had crossed trails with down through the years. "Don't ever give him an even break, Rufe," Jake had warned. "He can't be beat."

Scott Lerda now said, "Lonnie, you and Ira and Jules stay here. The rest of you go back over to the livery stable and take another look for Jake. I know damned well he's there somewhere."

Antrim dismounted, lowering his bridle reins. So did Ira Purkey, who was scrawny, with stooped shoulders and sunken cheeks. Jules Hahn swung down, too, carrying a rope. He was a fat man with flabby jowls and a head with a high, narrow dome. One of the others said, *"Vamonos,"* and all reined their horses around to ride toward the plaza, passing between the saloon building and that of the barbershop.

Meeting Lerda's cruel gaze, Tolliver said, "Go easy on Mawson. Don't blame him for what I did."

"I'll go easy on him—after he explains why he sat there and let you gun Bill down."

"Jake Mawson practically raised me, fellow. I tagged around after him all the time when I was a button, and he'd do anything for me."

Lerda sneered. "He took sides. And killed Ben

Gregory to keep Gregory from giving Bill a hand. Gregory would have tallied you for shooting my brother if it hadn't been for Jake. Let him explain that to me."

Tolliver watched him silently. Gesturing at his dusty clothes, Tolliver said then, "Why rough me up like this, Lerda? Why don't you fight me like a man?"

"You'll get what's coming to you."

"Let me have it now, then. What are you waiting on?"

Lerda grinned. "I want the old man around to watch me settle with you."

"All right," Tolliver said. "Let me know when you find him." He started to walk off.

Lerda clutched at him, saying, "Hold on, there." Jerking free, Tolliver swung a fist that smacked on Lerda's stubbled jaw. Lerda went backward and landed on his shoulders, gun half-drawn. One of the men behind Tolliver voiced a startled oath. Before either of the men at his back could seize him, Tolliver sprang forward and stamped down on Lerda's gun hand. He stooped to retrieve Lerda's weapon, but Purkey, or Hahn, grasped his cartridge belt and yanked him backward, and Antrim hit him over the head with a gun barrel. Tolliver went down. Jules Hahn kicked him in the side and struck at his face with the folded rope.

Lerda got to his feet and inspected his six-shooter,

giving its cylinder a spin. "I'll pacify him," he said savagely, and stood over Tolliver with the gun muzzle bearing on Tolliver's brow. Tolliver lunged forward in an attempt to throw his arms around Lerda's legs to bring him down, every muscle in him braced for the shock of Lerda's slug. The renegade didn't shoot. Swiftly reversing the weapon, he brought the butt down on Tolliver's bare head. As Tolliver slipped into oblivion against a background of honky-tonk noises from the Desert Star, he heard Scott Lerda growl, "Killing's too damn good for him."

When he regained consciousness, he was trussed up, lying on the rammed-earth floor of the *jacal* not far from the corner fireplace, which wasn't in use at this season. A couple of deer-hide carpets, two cane-bottomed chairs and a settee and a blanket-covered mattress folded against one wall were the only furnishings. Tolliver noticed, too, a religious *nicho* decorated with paper flowers, bits of lace and ribbon, and the room was clean, as though recently tidied up by *Mexicanas*.

Tolliver's hands were behind his back, his wrists bound by a pigging string, and the Lerda gang had half-hitched his legs with a lasso. Closing his eyes again, he heard a mutter of voices in the *cocina*, the hut's only other room, and tried to distinguish what the owl hoots were saying. He couldn't. He lay there with his teeth clenched against the pounding ache behind his eyes. The wound given him by Gregory was throbbing again, as though reopened by the pistol-whipping from Antrim and Lerda.

The men in the kitchen seemed to be counting money.

Fingers tingling, Tolliver began flexing them to restore circulation. After a time he rolled toward the folded mattress and managed to get upon it, but his spurs made a racket that brought Jules Hahn to the inner doorway. Hahn stood there watching him intently, without Tolliver being aware of it, and then the fat-faced renegade turned back into the kitchen.

Tolliver heard him say to Antrim, "He just wasn't comfortable, Lonnie."

Antrim said only, "Pour me some of that *aguardiente*, Jules," and glassware tinkled.

With memory returning fully, Tolliver found himself unable to repress a groan. Walt Sprague had been waiting for him at the sheriff's office, and he hadn't made it. What would Sheriff Stroud do now? Nothing. Alone, he and Sprague wouldn't be capable of doing anything. None of the townsfolk or the lower valley ranchers would give Stroud a hand, either. In view of Tolliver's shooting Bill Lerda, and considering the unsavory rumors that Tolliver might even be a rustler himself, no one in Eagle Bend would risk his life in taking Tolliver's part against Scott Lerda and these other renegades. *I've got to get out of here,* Tolliver thought.

Rolling over face-down on the mattress, Tolliver strained against the bond which secured his wrists. They were unyielding.

He relaxed, breathing deeply for a while, and tried again. Still he couldn't budge the pigging string. Without help, he told himself, he would never get loose. The more he struggled against them, the tighter grew the knots which held him.

He lay for a time, resting, listening; but could detect no change in the roundabout noises of the settlement—the honkytonk noises, blacksmith shop sounds, wagon hubs knocking along the street in front of the saloon, and the cawing of a crow; then from the kitchen came Jules Hahn's voice:

"If he took out down the valley, he's headed for the Pecos and the Guadalupes. Scott'll keep after him till he catches him."

"Seems to me," the kid said, "that Scott's going to a lot of trouble just to get even with the old man."

"Scott's recollecting Devils River and Jake threatening to kill Bill. He figures Jake put Tolliver up to gunning Bill, because Bill never was a hand to let a split-tail girl get him into a jackpot."

"Scott don't believe that Hashim woman was making a deal with Bill?"

"No. With all this dinero, what in hell would Bill want to go to work for?"

Moving his head to look at the kitchen doorway,

Tolliver said, "Hey, you in there, come here a minute."

The flabby-jowled Hahn appeared first, the kid behind him, and both had a handful of banknotes.

The kid said, "What do you want, Tolliver?"

"Let me make a deal with you."

"No deal," the kid said, sneering, and turned to go back into the *cocina.*

"Hold on," Tolliver said. "Listen to what I've got to say. Scott's wrong about Mawson. The old man didn't know a thing about that ruckus. Mark Connick was behind it—at least, behind Ben Gregory's part. Connick was hoping to get Gregory killed, and he succeeded. Now he's up there taking charge of the Bar G ranch. If somebody doesn't stop him, he'll be in a position to write checks on the Gregory account pretty soon, and he'll put together a crew of gunmen that'll make you fellows look sick. He hates Scott Lerda even worse than he does me, and the first thing he'll look for will be a showdown with all of you. He'll wipe you out, too."

Antrim and Hahn exchanged glances. Sarcastically Hahn said, "But you wouldn't if you had a chance to, would you, *amigo?*"

The pale-eyed kid studied Tolliver thoughtfully. Finally he said, "You're a mighty smooth talker, but why should we look to you to do something about Connick's plans? First time he shows up in town, Scott will tend to him. Scott would have done it long ago if Connick hadn't begged with tears in his eyes."

"Where is Scott?" Tolliver asked.

"He's trying to catch the old man. Mawson lit a shuck for other parts, and Scott and the others took out after him." Dropping his gaze to the banknotes in his fist, the kid jerked his head at Hahn, and the two went back into the kitchen.

Tolliver again set grimly to work to free his hands. Apparently each wrist had been tied separately and then both bound together, and as the day wore on he decided it was futile to struggle. He might have freed his legs, but his spurs made a racket that brought his guards looking in on him. Finally Hahn threatened to buffalo him if he didn't lie still, and Tolliver relaxed, knowing it would avail him nothing to be bludgeoned senseless again.

A dark-haired, olive-skinned *Mexicana,* one bright black eye concealed by a *rebozo,* came in presently and knelt beside him to feed him a supper of beans and *tortillas.*

While eating, he asked, "How can a lovely little thing like you connive with a bunch of thieving killers to keep me tied up here?"

"Every little dove has her gall, *senor.*"

"If you'll help me get away from here," Tolliver said, "I'll buy you everything you can think of. I'll deck you out like a little queen."

"*Guapo.*"

When he had finished his supper and the *senorita*

had let him smoke a cigarette, he asked again, "Why don't you help me get out of here?"

"It does not please me."

"You're not afraid to," Tolliver said. "Scott wouldn't harm you. If he lost the backing of the Mexicans, he'd be finished."

"Of the *ladrones, senor*," the girl said stiffly. She left the room.

Hahn and Antrim were playing poker. They had been playing all afternoon, and now continued the game until darkness came on. Lamplight shone in the kitchen. Hahn said, "We ought to have the light in yonder, Lonnie. How'll we play cards—move the table in there?"

"Can't move a two-legged table, Jules."

"Fastened to the wall, eh? I never noticed."

They were still for a time, and Tolliver heard Antrim say, "Well, keep your eye on those saddlebags, and I'll go borrow a lamp."

"Bring a bottle of tequila or something, too, kid."

"I'm not going to the saloon—just next door. You heard what Scott said. He told us to stay away from there. And he meant for us not to do any drinking here."

"Yeah, I know," Hahn said. "I've had enough, anyway. Hurry up and get the lamp."

Coming into the living room, the kid stopped to inspect Tolliver's bonds, and went on out. It was a lantern he returned with. He set it on the floor near the fireplace. Reconsidering, he took it clear across the room, and Tolliver expelled a breath of disappointment, his mind already having seized upon the hope of using the flame to burn the thongs off his wrists.

Later, listening to the sporadic talk between the poker players, he heard Hahn say, "We'll miss Mawson, Lonnie."

"I won't."

"Hadn't been for him," Hahn said, "these saddlebags wouldn't be stuffed with dinero."

"Mawson didn't plan it, did he?"

"No. But he came in mighty handy. One of those fellows had a point-blank drop on Scott's brisket, but the old man downed him before he could shoot. I aim to remind Scott of that when he gets back, if he brings Mawson with him."

"According to Bill," Antrim said, "the old man's been helping himself to more than his share. You'd better not remind Scott of anything. I can't open it, Jules; deal another hand."

Tolliver kept listening for hoofbeats that would announce Scott Lerda's return, and as the minutes dragged by, he found himself succumbing to hopelessness. Scott Lerda intended to kill him, and he was almost positive, too, that he would be right here, tied hand and foot, when Scott did return. It was useless to expect Walt Sprague and Sheriff Stroud to free him, unless they could muster help from the townspeople. Tolliver thought: Stroud knows what's going on, though. He knows that Scott took Jake's trail and that nothing will be done about me until those fellows get back.

The Desert Star revelry was a background to Tolliver's thoughts. When the tinny jangle of the piano, the twanging of the stringed instruments and the thump of the drum were silent, there was an occasional outburst of drunken laughter or a merry shriek from one of the girls. During the intervals of silence at the Desert Star and the Brass Rail on the opposite corner, Tolliver could hear the more remote sounds of the town and also the noise made by Antrim and Hahn in the kitchen—their talk, the fluttering noise of shuffled pasteboards, a scraping when they moved a boot, the tinkle of a rowel.

Then one tinkle, faint as it was, made Tolliver's heart pound. It brought his eyes wide open. Tense, he kept listening.

CHAPTER XVI

The tinkle hadn't come from the kitchen; it had reached Tolliver through an open window. He watched that window. It was a square of blackness; above and beyond it the limbs and leaves of a tree made a pattern against a starry sky. Slowly a high-peaked hat and a hard-set face appeared at the window. A yellow forelock showed beneath the hat—the darkly tanned, blue-eyed face of Bigelow, the cattle buyer. Seeing Tolliver on the fold of mattress and blanket across the room, Bigelow seemed startled. He withdrew from sight. Tolliver moistened his lips, a vein throbbing strong in his neck.

Bigelow moved back into sight, his tense gaze meeting that of Tolliver. In the cattle buyer's right fist was a six gun. With the forefinger of his left hand, he indicated the rear of the building. Tolliver's lips formed the word "two." Bigelow held up two fingers. Tolliver nodded.

It seemed then that Bigelow intended to turn back into the night, but at this instant Lonnie Antrim got up from the table and appeared in the doorway. He had heard a noise that aroused his suspicions, or it could have been a natural feral instinct that brought him.

At any rate, his gaze wasn't toward Tolliver. He saw Bigelow outside the window. Standing paralyzed for a second, he screamed, "No!" but the Colt in Bigelow's fist began exploding. Tolliver didn't count Bigelow's shots, but the yellow-haired man fired once after Antrim had gone down, and then he said savagely, "Squirm, if you're able to!"

Even as Bigelow's gun roared and his voice sounded, Tolliver heard Jules Hahn trying to escape through the back door, with more gunshots sounding behind the building.

Leaning on the windowsill, Bigelow called through the house, "Did you get him, Sprague?"

"Yeah, I got him, Mr. Bigelow. Just winged him."

"Bring him on," Bigelow ordered, and still stood there.

After a moment Sprague said, "Don't sull on me—get up!"

"Give him another slug," Bigelow said roughly.

"He's coming."

Bigelow came around to the door then, and entered the *jacal* to cut Tolliver's bonds. He kept his attention on the doorway of the kitchen.

Presently Jules Hahn appeared there, with Walt

Sprague holding a gun muzzle against his spine. Bleeding from a shoulder wound, Hahn's jowled visage was as white as a sheet, the man himself speechless with dread.

From the alley Sheriff Jim Stroud's voice called, "Tolliver all right, Chet?"

Bigelow turned his head, yelling, "Everything's fine, Jim."

"Kill both of them?"

"Antrim. Hahn's able to walk."

"Want me to come and get him?"

"I'll bring him." Moving from Tolliver to Antrim, the yellow-haired man slapped the dead man's pockets.

Hahn said hoarsely, "He ain't got none of it on him. Or me, either."

Sprague said, "It's in the kitchen, Mr. Bigelow. They've been playing poker with it."

"Just killing time till Scott gets back," Hahn said.

Standing erect, Bigelow said over his shoulder, "Scott's back." The cattle buyer entered the *cocina*. Hahn licked his lips, and stood there with bulging eyes as though stupefied by fear. Returning from the kitchen with a pair of saddlebags, Bigelow said to Sprague, "Give Tolliver a hand." Bigelow himself gave Jules Hahn a shove toward the front of the room. "Get moving. Right straight through there to the plaza."

As the cattle buyer followed his prisoner out, Sprague asked, "Are you through with me, Mr. Bigelow?"

Bigelow glanced around. "We told you what to do, didn't we?"

"Yeah."

Tolliver was rubbing the furrows where the thongs had dug into his wrists. "What did he tell you to do?"

"Help Lurelle," Sprague said.

Holstering his gun, the Bar G waddy looked down at Tolliver until Tolliver made a move toward rising.

There was no feeling in Tolliver's legs, and he thought he was still tied, thought he couldn't get up.

Sprague said, "Here—catch hold of me."

With Sprague's help, Tolliver gained his feet, but he couldn't take a step—only stood there trying to work circulation back into his muscles.

"Bigelow said Lerda's back. Stroud got him?"

"Yeah. Lerda and three of his men."

"Bigelow helping the sheriff?"

Sprague nodded. "He just got back to town a little while ago, or we'd of been here sooner. Me and the sheriff tried all day to raise a posse and didn't have any luck. Sheriff Stroud said there was no use in me and him tackling Antrim and Hahn without help— just to get ourselves killed."

Having moved around enough to make his muscles respond normally, Tolliver went over to Antrim's body. "Did you pick up my hat and guns, Walt?"

"I didn't, but somebody else did. They're over in Stroud's office."

Tolliver had pulled a six-shooter from the dead man's holster. Tossing it back down, he said, "Bring your horse?"

Sprague nodded.

"Well, let's go over to Stroud's place and get my own gun."

Stepping out into the alley, Tolliver was instantly aware that the Desert Star, although well lighted, was silent and appeared deserted. The usual noises from the Brass Rail, on the opposite corner, no longer filled the night, either. The entire town was silent; then Tolliver heard an ax blow, followed by the ring of other axes, as though several men were chopping wood.

"What are they doing—building a bonfire on the plaza?"

Sprague said, "Uh-huh."

Tolliver started toward the passageway between the Desert Star building and the barber shop.

Sprague said, "Here's my horse, around here, Tolliver."

"I'm all right now. I can walk."

"Wait a minute, Tolliver. Ain't nothing been done about Lurelle, and Stroud wants you and me to light out up there."

Sprague felt in a pocket and dug out a piece of metal which glinted in the light from the *jacal*. "He deputized me and said the county would pay all expenses. Told me to get you to help me and go right to Mark Connick and put him under arrest. The sheriff said if I could bring Connick to town, he would pistol-whip a confession out of him about Morgan Hashim's bushwhacking."

"Got guts enough to try that?"

"I have, if you'll go with me."

"Sure, I will," Tolliver said. "Let's go over and get my guns and a horse."

They rode Sprague's mount double around the north side of the Desert Star and passed in front of the Brass Rail, where men on the porch gazed silently toward the plaza. Also looking toward the square, faintly illuminated by lampshine which drifted out from the surrounding business places and from a small bonfire blaze near the water trough, Tolliver saw a sizable crowd, mounted and dismounted; and light-colored clothes here and there told him that several among the gathering were women.

"Created quite a bit of excitement," Tolliver commented.

He and Sprague rode on past the saddlery. Nearing Stroud's gate, the Bar G hand said, "You stay put, Tolliver. I'll get your hat and guns."

"Get some extra cartridges too," Tolliver said, and Sprague dismounted.

The Bar G hand disappeared toward Jim Stroud's patio, and when he returned with Tolliver's belongings, Mrs. Stroud followed him to the gate. Sprague was saying to her, "Yes, Jim is plumb all right, ma'am."

The sheriff's wife stood in the gateway and greeted Tolliver, and was concerned with him, too. He assured her that he was all right, and said then, "I've been doing a lot of thinking about you and Jim today, and I want you to give him a talking to. Make him quit wearing that star. Take him back over into New Mexico to that little ranch he was telling me about."

Felicia said, "Someone has to wear the star, or the *bandidos* will drive us from our homes."

"That's right, but Jim doesn't have to wear it."

"He's not forced to, Tolliver, but he likes to. And the people want him to. He's a good sheriff, no? Thees valley will be peaceful soon."

"Of course he's a good sheriff, ma'am, but good sheriffs die, too. Jim's a family man; make him do what I said." Sprague had handed Tolliver his guns and hat, and was back in the saddle now, so Tolliver told him, "Let's hurry it up."

When they had taken leave of the sheriff's wife, they rode up the street in front of the restaurant, where another silent group of townsfolk stood and gazed toward the square, kept at a distance by Jim Stroud.

Reining up at the corral gate of the Plaza Feed and Sale Stable, Tolliver and Sprague found the hostler coming off the porch to meet them.

Tolliver said, "Got a horse I can ride forty-five miles before daylight? I don't want to take that Mule-shoe buckskin I stabled here."

"I've got two or three that'll carry you there, Tolliver. How did you make out—come through that scrape all right?"

"All right so far," Tolliver said.

Entering the corral with the stableman, he got his saddle and blanket and bridle out of the tack room, sliding his carbine into the boot, and he waited for the hostler to rope him a mount. The ring of axes still sounded on the plaza as men continued to chop firewood, and the bonfire itself was getting larger and larger. Sizing up the mustang the stableman led toward him, Tolliver asked, "Isn't that pony a little too small for me?"

"This horse'll carry your weight better than any other bronc in this lot. He's rough-gaited, though. When you get there, you'll be in worse shape than him."

"I don't care about that, just so I get there, me and Walt."

Leading the saddled horse outside and mounting, Tolliver said, "Want to grab a bite to eat before we go?"

"No," Sprague said, "let's ride. Let's get there as quick as we can."

Back on the porch now, the stableman said, "Well, Tolliver, I'm going to miss the old man's talking about what you and him aimed to do up there in the Dragoon Hills."

"What's that you said?"

"I was just thinking," the stableman said vaguely, and was silent.

Tolliver looked at Walt Sprague. He glanced toward the activities on the plaza, and then said harshly to the hostler, "What about Mawson?"

The stableman said nothing.

Shifting uneasily in his saddle, Walt Sprague said wearily, "Go ahead. You've spilled the beans. Tell him what's going on."

The stableman said lamely, "I thought he already knew."

Facing Walt Sprague, Tolliver said, "Just trying to toll me out of town, huh?"

Sprague expelled a long breath. "No. Lurelle needs help, Tolliver—all alone up there with Connick and Kelse and Jepsen and them fellows. She called on you for help, and if she doesn't get it, what'll she think? That you're no good."

Tolliver was angered through and through but not so quick-tempered or hot-headed that he couldn't follow Walt Sprague's line of reasoning. Sprague was right. If Tolliver didn't go to her when she needed him, Lurelle would consider him afraid to. She had grown to womanhood with a hard-case crew of hands around her, and she had only contempt for a weakling. Also, losing faith in Tolliver, she would question the truth of what he had told her about Mark Connick. She might even willingly strike out somewhere with Connick to marry him.

Tolliver said, "What is Jim Stroud doing out there, Walt—getting ready to throw a necktie party?"

"That's right, Tolliver. They aim to hang the old man and Scott Lerda and Ira Purkey."

"And Jules Hahn," Tolliver.

"Yeah."

Trying to force himself to relax, Tolliver said, "Well, Walt, you can do whatever you want to, but I've got to help old Jake Mawson. He practically raised me."

Reining around, Tolliver rode straight onto the plaza, toward the crowd near the bonfire. Fanny Hashim and Cheryl were there, in divided riding skirts and range clothes, sitting their mounts between those of Phillips and Sturdivant. Half a dozen others were mounted, but the rest of the crowd had either left their saddles or had gathered here afoot. Tolliver saw several Eagle Bend businessmen standing around, but no one seemed to be here just as a spectator.

Scott Lerda and the three members of his gang were sitting their saddles under a big live oak not far from the water trough, Lerda with blood on the lower part of his face. Several townsmen were hunkered over a coil of hemp, cutting four ropes of equal length and getting ready to soap them. Sheriff Stroud and Bigelow and Hutton were standing together looking on, and the rest of Bigelow's crew were holding guns on the prisoners.

"Have you gone plumb wild, Sheriff?" Tolliver demanded, swinging down beside the lawman.

"No, I don't reckon."

"You're sworn to uphold the law, and mob violence isn't the law."

"I don't see no mob."

"They haven't had a court trial."

A sly edge to his voice, the sheriff said, "No, they haven't, but what can I do about it?"

"Get some sense, Sheriff. Take these men over in Tom Green County and hold them for trial."

"Will you help me?"

"Sure, I'll help you."

The yellow-haired cattle buyer said, "Jim Stroud's not doing the calling for this dance."

"Who is?"

"I am."

Tolliver took a couple of steps forward and found himself confronted by Hutton, too.

Bigelow said, "I lost a thousand head of longhorn cattle to these Eagle Bend killers down on Devils River a while back."

"What did you do with the money in those saddle-bags?" Tolliver demanded.

"It's mine," Bigelow said. "It's pay for my steers. But I haven't collected for my men—five good ones, shot down in cold blood. They were more important than the cattle, and that's why I came here. It would take every renegade in this valley to square off for my hands."

He and Tolliver locked gazes.

"You're not including Jake Mawson," Tolliver said. "He was running from the Lerda gang. Didn't you know that?"

"He was running from me, too, Tolliver."

"He didn't do any running at the Muleshoe. As a matter of fact, he could have killed you. So that shows he wasn't guilty of what you claim."

"With that Bar G slug in him," Bigelow said, "he didn't feel like making a run for it. Besides that, he was counting on you to do his fighting."

"I guess that's the reason he knocked Ben Gregory over."

Bigelow was silent. Some of the onlookers backed away a few paces, ready to hurl themselves to the ground if gunfire broke out. In the taut silence, the stamping and switching of the horses and the jingle of their bit chains seemed loud. Some of the broncs were working their bit crickets. One of the towns-men, calmly disregarding the hazards, shouldered his ax to tackle a log dragged in at the end of a lariat.

Tolliver went over to look at Scott Lerda. "No point in holding a grudge against the old man now, Scott. Tell them the truth about him; tell them he had no part of any rustling or killing."

Even as he spoke, Tolliver knew he was asking Scott Lerda to save the old man's neck with a lie. Tolliver had gleaned enough from the talk between Antrim and Hahn to know that. Jake had not only participated in the rustling down on Devils River; he had shot at least one of Bigelow's trail hands, the one who Hahn said had a bead on Scott Lerda himself. A word from Lerda now would free old Jake, and if the owl-hoot chief knew of Jake's saving his life, he might speak up. It would be irony, however, to ask Hahn to tell what he knew, for Mawson's guilt would then be apparent to all.

Scott leaned sidewise to spit when Tolliver addressed him, parting his lips with obvious difficulty. One side of his whiskered jaw was matted with dried blood, Tolliver noticed. The renegade held his silence.

Bigelow said, "He can't talk, Tolliver. Got shot in the mouth."

"Did you kill those other fellows?" Tolliver asked, moving nearer.

"Don't see them around anywhere, do you?" Bigelow countered sarcastically.

Tolliver's eyes smoldered. "Turn Mawson loose, Bigelow. Chances are you stole those cattle they took from you. At least some of them. And your men had a fighting chance."

Old Jake Mawson himself said, "Son, you're getting all worked up. Don't play your string out, too."

"Who's playing his string out?" Tolliver asked. He made a move that placed Bigelow's five gun hands into his range of vision and in the same instant jerked his own gun, angling its muzzle directly at the fancy-dressed cattle buyer.

"Hadn't been for me, you'd be dead now!" Bigelow cried.

"I don't owe you a thing, Bigelow!"

Five of Bigelow's six trail hands were holding six guns and could easily have snapped slugs at Tolliver, but Tolliver's finger had already tripped his trigger and he was holding the hammer of the Colt back with his thumb. Even a shot directed at the frame of Tolliver's weapon itself would have been risky for Bigelow. Bigelow's men continued to point their six-shooters at the mounted prisoners, whose horses they were holding.

"Scott's brother wasn't a bit afraid of you, Bigelow," Tolliver continued. "He saw you sashaying around town here. My idea is he was all set to chouse you back where you came from. Tallying Bill Lerda was a favor to you, and it makes us even."

Bigelow sneered. "You're right—two of a kind."

Hutton said, "Chet, I told you Tolliver was one of them, but you said you were sure of him."

"I'm still sure of him. He's no cow thief—just a damned fool."

"Think he'll shoot if we try to take his gun?"

"No, he won't shoot," Bigelow said.

From her saddle Cheryl Hashim said in a choked tone, "He will, too, Chet."

Tense silence held.

Fanny Hashim said, "Don't risk it, Bigelow. Don't underrate him. Ask Jim Stroud whether he'll shoot or not. Jim told him to go over to the Desert Star and shoot Bill Lerda, and he went right over there and did it."

Startled by Mrs. Hashim's bluntless, Sheriff Stroud glanced furtively around at the townspeople, and said gruffly, "I feel justified. Something drastic had to be done about that daughter of yours, Fanny. But this here is different. Tolliver is in the wrong here."

Tolliver said, "Damned if that's so."

"It's different and much more serious, Jim," Fanny Hashim said. "Tolliver and Mawson are the same as kinfolks." She put her gaze back on the cattle buyer. "I've seen more trouble than you have, and I can smell it farther. Do as Tolliver says, or this daughter of mine will be crying her eyes out over you."

Fanny Hashim was backing Tolliver's play because she felt she owed it to him, and Bigelow was paying heed to her, respecting her opinion because she was the mother of the girl he'd fallen in love with.

Suddenly, hearing spur-clad boots approaching from a direction not within his range of vision as he kept Bigelow and the other men under surveillance, Tolliver's features twisted with disappointment. Someone coming up behind him would nullify the advantage he held here. It was Walt Sprague, though. "Steady, Tolliver," he said, and stopped walking. He seemed to be sizing up the situation. "I'll go get my horse," he said then, and trotted away. Hoofbeats announced his return. "Bring your horse around behind Mawson's, Tolliver, and we'll get gone."

Hoarsely Jules Hahn said, "Take us with you."

Sprague ignored him.

"Walt Sprague, don't forget you're my deputy," Stroud said angrily.

"I'm a Bar G hand first of all, Jim, and Lurelle told me to bring Tolliver up there. I aim to do it if it harelips every badge-toter in Texas."

Disgusted, Stroud said, "How can a county sheriff do anything? Everybody wants the law enforced, but only against the other fellow."

"Trouble is, Jim, the law generally sets on the fence and jumps off on the side he figures is the strongest. You just stand hitched like the rest of them, or I'll let Mr. Bigelow have it. He makes the best target around here."

Tolliver had mounted his horse and taken the reins of Mawson's bronc from Bigelow's man. The fellow was gripping a six-shooter, but resistance, he knew, would only get Chet Bigelow shot down. There was too much to lose and too little to gain at the moment, Bigelow having already recovered the price of his rustled steers.

"Mrs. Hashim," Tolliver said, "I'm much obliged for that camping outfit and use of the horses. Your buckskin is over in the Plaza corral, but I don't know what happened to your filly."

"I do," Bigelow said. "That old man shot it through the head and got behind its carcass when we closed in on him."

Tolliver said, "I'll replace her, ma'am."

"Don't worry about it, Tolliver," Fanny Hashim told him. "It's not the first Muleshoe horse to die that way. Morgan had to do that now and then, when the Comanches were depredating."

Troy Sturdivant said, "You've got a horse in our roundup cavvy, Tolliver."

"I'll get it. Take your buckskin home, huh?"

"All right."

Fanny said, "*Adios*, if I don't see you again, Tolliver."

Tolliver said dryly, "No hopes of that, ma'am. I'll be around here for a long time yet."

A moment later, he and Sprague, hipping around in their saddles with the oldster's horse jogging along between theirs, rode off the square. They would have been sitting ducks for Bigelow's guns, but they headed toward the lights of the Brass Rail. A fusillade directed at them would have endangered those on the saloon porch and perhaps others out there in the darkness, for all the men on the plaza could tell. Her choked voice carrying far in the silence, Cheryl said, "Don't you dare, Chet Bigelow! Let them go, or it will never end." She was referring, of course, to the upper-valley war, thinking of herself and Bigelow on one bank of the Dragoon, Tolliver and Lurelle on the other—the same stage, the same old tragedy; just a different cast.

Tolliver and Mawson and the Bar G hand rode around the northeast wall of the Brass Rail, cutting through a weed patch, and then changed their course in order to place the saloon building between themselves and the crowd around the bonfire on the square. Stopping briefly, Tolliver and Sprague both dismounted, Tolliver cutting the oldster's wrists loose from the saddle horn and Sprague freeing his legs of the rope which encircled the barrel of his mount.

"Stop any more slugs, Jake?"

"No. None touched me, boy. It was a right smart shindig while it lasted. They'd have tallied me if I hadn't given up. Bigelow seen Scott and them fellows overtake me, and he waylaid us on the way back to town."

"Able to stick on this horse?"

"For a while. I sure don't want to be decorating that live oak back yonder with them other fellows."

Sprague lifted his bandanna to wipe his perspiring face. "Reckon they'll trail us?"

"Not anyways soon. Bigelow'll have a hard time slipping off from Cheryl."

Mounting again, Tolliver led the way into the night, traveling at a jog trot except when slowed by a gully or a motte of brush. There was no moonlight yet to skyline them. Climbing to a hogback that veered toward the river, Tolliver rode along it until it sloped into the *bosque* which fringed the Dragoon. Stopping to survey the town for a moment and listening intently, he heard no pursuit and went on down into the timber, dismounting in a small natural clearing. He rolled and lit a cigarette. Sprague and Mawson ground-tied their horses near his.

Sprague said, "I was thinking about what you told the stableman. You wanted a horse able to reach the Bar G by daylight. Don't you think it'll be too tough a ride for Mr. Mawson?"

Instantly old Jake growled, "I'm not going to the Bar G."

Both Sprague and Tolliver looked at him in the darkness.

"What's on your mind, Jake?"

"I'll do better by myself, son. I'll watch my chances and get out of this cussed valley, and then I'll rattle my hocks toward El Paso. I've got bank money in El Paso and own a piece of property there. No law from these parts will ever touch me."

"Sounds all right, Jake," Tolliver said thoughtfully. "You'll have to cross the river. What are you going to do about grub? You haven't got any guns, either."

"I'll make out, boy."

Unbuckling his cartridge belt, Tolliver nudged the oldster with it and his holstered six gun.

"You'll need it yourself."

"Go ahead and put it on," Tolliver said, and afterward changed the carbine from his saddle boot to Mawson's.

Jake said, "Don't worry now, boy. I'll make it fine. I can live on game if I have to." He gathered up his bridle reins.

"Leaving us now, Jake?"

"Yeah. It's best for me to go it alone." Saddle leather creaked as the oldster swung up and brush crackled as he rode slowly toward the main channel of the Dragoon. Tolliver stood motionless, facing in that direction, and presently there was silence. Mawson had reined in.

"*Vaya con Dios,* Rufe," he called.

Parting stiff lips to tell the old man good-by was a difficult thing to do, for some reason, Tolliver discovered.

CHAPTER XVII

Walt Sprague rolled and smoked a cigarette, too, standing with Tolliver as the sounds of Mawson's progress receded farther and farther into the depths of the *bosque*. "If the old man aims to cross the river," Sprague mused, "he's headed the wrong way. Gets deeper that way."

"Jake knows it, too," Tolliver said.

"Maybe that business about El Paso was just talk," Sprague reflected. "On account of me. Mawson probably doesn't trust me any farther than he can see me."

"If he doesn't, who would he trust? You saved his neck. Jake probably isn't ready to cross the river yet. It could be that the money he mentioned isn't in El Paso, and he aims to dig it up and take it with him."

"Well, I don't blame him for that. I would. Money stashed in a hollow log won't help anybody." Losing interest in the old man, Sprague said, "Hadn't we better get going?"

"Walt," Tolliver asked, "would you shy away from going back to town alone?"

"No, I don't think so," Sprague said, after considering it. "Jim Stroud knows why I stuck my bill in. Him and me's been worrying about Lurelle all day. No, he won't hold nothing against me. Why do you ask?"

"Because I want you to go back down there and hire some hands. For me. I can't speak for the Bar G."

"Gun hands?"

"Gun hands if they've got cow savvy. I want men who are interested in steady jobs."

"Aim to start running cattle up there in the hills?"

"Sometime."

"Bucking Connick," Sprague reflected, as if to himself. "Those fellows who quit the Circle C might be willing to do that, Tolliver. They know Mark Connick is wrong and hate his guts."

"Talk to them."

"Then what?"

"If you can shape up any crew at all, head for the Bar G. Because I'll sure be needing some backing."

"You can count on it. Mawson took your guns. You can have mine, and I'll stop by Jim Stroud's place and get some more."

"I could be wrong," Tolliver said. "Bigelow might already be sniffing our trail. And if you were to meet up with him—"

"I could high-tail it."

"I won't have any call to use a gun between here and the Bar G," Tolliver said, "and when I get there I'll probably have to lay low until you catch up with me."

"It would be kind of foolish to tackle Connick and Kelse and them fellows without a *corrida* at your back. Lurelle would be in a worse fix than ever if you got yourself put out of commission."

"She'd make out somehow. But it's like you say— no use proving Bigelow right about my being a fool," Tolliver said.

A few minutes later he had lifted his horse into a hard gallop along the well-marked trail to the ranch on the river's east bank in the north end of the valley. He held steadily to the gait and stopped only to let the horse blow. Afterward he went on foot for a ways.

He had only starlight to guide him when he crossed Laguna Creek and the trail which led to his place in the Dragoon Hills. By the time he reached the live-oak knolls and long grassy flats surrounding the headquarters buildings of the Gregory ranch, weird light from a half-hidden moon had turned the timber along the river into a leafy, impenetrable wall. It cast a silver sheen over the waterless sand hills to the east and outlined the bluntly serrated, high-flung edge of the Llano Estacado yonder against the north.

Within sight of the Gregory cemetery knoll, Tolliver turned his horse into the river bosque, toward a natural clearing he remembered. He intended to unsaddle his mount and stake it out where it could reach water. Dubious of what lay ahead, he changed his mind and turned the horse loose. The men at the Plaza corral fed their stock grain; maybe this critter would go back where it came from. If not, Tolliver would round him up later, and now was no time to worry about piling up a livery stable bill.

Tolliver wondered about his spurs but decided to keep them on. Insects, night birds and frogs lifted a shrill, hoarse din in the brush tangles of the marshy river bottom as Tolliver considered the chore ahead. According to Walt Sprague, Connick had forbidden Lurelle to leave the ranch. Lurelle, of course, knew Connick wanted only to keep her away from Tolliver Connick had posted guards. It seemed unlikely he would keep the girl herself under surveillance. A woman appreciated rivalry for her hand, up to a point. Lurelle would tolerate Connick so long as he didn't mistreat her. A guard placed over her person, though, would be gross mistreatment, and would lose Connick whatever regard the girl held for him, if any. No girl would strike out afoot from this isolated spot, and risk an encounter with a proddy range bull, so Connick hadn't placed Lurelle herself under restraint. He was just keeping the saddle horses away from her.

Following along the edge of the bosque to a point

nearest the shake-roofed log ranch house, Tolliver started directly toward it, more intensely alert than he would have been if packing a gun. Not a glimmer of light shone anywhere, no glow of a cigarette, no sign at all of anyone's being awake and watchful. Tolliver stepped upon the front gallery. He found the door shut; it was also locked. Tolliver relaxed. Lurelle was inside alone, and fearful.

Moving to a window, Tolliver found it shut tight. He lifted the sash carefully and felt around for the age-slick peeled-willow prop, leaving the window raised after he had stepped over the sill. He was standing in the carpeted living room. Straight across was the door to Ben Gregory's small office, and the door to the hallway was on the right; the house was silent except for the ticking clocks.

Unable to see, Tolliver felt a path across the room and into the hall, stomach muscles braced for a bullet, but he had scarcely stepped from the living room when Lurelle cried in a terror-choked voice, "You get out of here!" She had changed bedrooms.

"Don't be scared—it's me."

"Rufe! Oh—!" She rushed into the hallway and threw herself into his arms, weeping.

"Reckon they'll hear you?"

She grew silent, but continued to sob, her shoulders shaking. Having found her fully clothed, Tolliver suspected she'd been afraid to drop off to sleep. Gently he stroked her hair. After a bit, drawing an unsteady breath, she lifted her arms, pulled his head down and kissed him. "Don't ever leave me again."

"I was afraid you'd hear me coming in and shoot me."

She had no gun. Connick had cleaned the ranch house out, removing even the old cap-and-ball navy Colts from over the mantelpiece.

"Haven't you slept any?"

"I sleep in the daytime."

"Looks like you would smother with the house shut up so tight," he said, and drew her into the living room. "Come on and sit down and tell me what happened."

She didn't have much to tell. Connick had told her he intended to hold her prisoner until Tolliver had been killed; then they would get married. "I thought you weren't coming," she said.

"Did Connick know you sent Walt Sprague after me?"

"I don't think so. Several of the men left. Connick got money to pay them. He sent some of them over onto the Muleshoe range to find you and shoot you. They never did come back. Connick and Kelse were talking about it. Kelse thought the Muleshoe killed them."

"The Muleshoe didn't. They just kept going, to get away from this mess."

Tolliver told her about the Lerda gang, what he'd

been up against, and before he finished, the Bar G headquarters was astir with the usual before-dawn activity.

"Connick'll be up here pretty soon, won't he?"

"No."

"Doesn't he come around you at all?"

"I scratched his face."

The cookshack triangle rang out. Lurelle stood up immediately. "He sent my breakfast yesterday morning. I'd better go light a lamp in the kitchen so he won't become suspicious."

Starting to turn away, she asked, "No telling when Walt will get here with those men, is there?"

"If he met up with Bigelow's outfit, he won't bring any men. Walt thinks Jim Stroud'll help him, but I figure Stroud'll take the deputy badge away from him and tell him to go to hell. Bigelow won't let Walt do anything that'll be of help to us. Bigelow'll figure old Jake Mawson's still with me, and he'll know I sent Walt back to town for something. We'll just have to help ourselves, Lurelle."

"What'll you do without a gun?"

"You iron clothes around here, don't you?"

"Clothes?"

"Give me one of your irons, and whoever brings your breakfast will get knocked in the head."

"They're in the kitchen."

"Get one of them before you light a lamp."

Tolliver followed her along the hallway, and took the iron from her at the kitchen door, stepping back out of sight as she struck a match.

Afterward he told her, "Do whatever you were doing this time yesterday morning."

She glanced past him along the hall. Daylight was showing above the timber along the Dragoon. "About this time," she said, "I opened the doors and raised some windows. Then I went out to the wash-bench and didn't come back in until Dobbs brought my breakfast."

Tolliver nodded.

"Rufe," the girl said, "Mark Connick is mean, every bit as mean as you told me he was."

He said nothing to that. When she had gone out onto the back gallery, he surveyed the kitchen but decided to stay in the hall. If Dobbs brought Lurelle's food, he wouldn't be expecting trouble. Off guard when Tolliver rushed him he might not get his gun out. Tolliver heard Lurelle working the pump. He listened to the *remuda* come in. Boots with clanking spurs clumped onto the back porch finally.

"Ma'am, you'd better make your peace with Mark. He ain't no man to fool with."

"I'm beginning to realize that, Gil."

Big of frame, insolent featured, Dobbs strode on into the kitchen to set a small coffeepot on the cookstove and to put a food tray down on the table. Lurelle entered behind him and lingered near the door, using a towel with trembling fingers. Dobbs glanced at her. He started to say something. At this instant Tolliver moved. Dobbs whirled, crouched and screeched a prolonged "Ah!" as he clawed for his six-gun. Tolliver struck him. Dobbs dropped, sprawling on the puncheons.

"Get inside, Lurelle."

With Dobbs' six-shooter in his fingers, Tolliver peered over a windowsill, watching the men in the area between the cookshack and the horse corral. He saw nothing to indicate they had heard Gil's squall.

Tolliver remained at the window for a long while and when he turned away, he knew that his enemies out there were Connick, Kelse, Jepsen and four others. He had no quarrel with the *remudero* or even with the cranky old cook.

Keeping low, Tolliver turned to the table and reached up for the lamp, bringing it to the floor before blowing it out. He replaced the lamp and hunkered over Dobbs, stripping him of his cartridge belt. The man was dead, so Tolliver dragged the body into a back bedroom and covered it with a sheet.

"You hit Gil too hard, Rufe."

"I'm out of practice, Lurelle."

Broad daylight covered the rangeland now. Reconnoitering again, Tolliver took the coffeepot and tray into the hall, where Lurelle sat cross-legged on the floor. He got dishes and silverware from the Gregory cupboard. He discovered then, despite the old *cocinero's* tight-fistedness with grub, that Lurelle hadn't been stinted. There was enough coffee, steak and gravy and sourdough biscuits for both of them. Rolling a smoke after sharing the girl's breakfast, Tolliver took another look around. It was sunrise, but none of the Bar G hands had caught up a horse yet. Standing at a rear window with narrowed eyes, Tolliver was speculating about this, and saw the heavy-jawed Kelse approaching the ranch house. Stopping quite a ways back, Kelse called, "Hey, Gil," and Tolliver drew the gun he'd taken from the man Kelse was hailing. He cocked the weapon, telling himself he would shoot the big foreman when Kelse got near enough for certain six-gun accuracy.

Kelse stood there for a minute or more looking at the house, and then he came on but all at once threw himself to the ground. In the same space of time a rifle roared, its slug sharding the windowpane over Tolliver's head. Someone had shot at him from inside the main barn. When Tolliver risked another look, Kelse was trotting toward the cookshack. Lifting the six-shooter as though taking aim at the moving Kelse, Tolliver jerked back from the window without firing, expecting another rifle shot. None came. He hadn't been seen. The first slug had been aimed at him by guesswork. Connick knew he was here.

It was mid-morning, with the Bar G cavvy still

penned in the corral, before Tolliver heard anything from Connick.

Coming up from the bunkhouse, Connick stopped near the blacksmith shed, where he could duck into the protection of its wall. "Tolliver," he shouted, "send Lurelle out of there if you don't want her to get hurt."

Tolliver glanced around. Lurelle shook her head and said, "No. I won't leave here without you."

"She doesn't want to come out, Connick."

Connick deliberated, his narrow-mustached face a blur of disappointment and hatred. "We can't flush you out of there with gunfire, but we'll get you tonight. We'll burn down the whole shebang. You hear me, Lurelle?"

Tolliver glanced around. She shook her head at him again, so he called through the window to Connick, "Lurelle said go ahead and burn it."

Connick gave the brim of his white hat a jerk. Muttering something in savage tone, he went back toward the bunkhouse, the colored inlays of his boot tops bright in the sunshine. Tolliver holstered his gun.

Lurelle said, "They must have seen you."

"I rode a livery-stable bronc and it came in with the cavvy. The Mexican probably cut sign on it and found my kak. He knows my saddle."

They moved back into the hall and hunkered

down, looking at each other with complete understanding. Tolliver rolled a smoke.

Lurelle said, "I sure hope Sprague brings those
men."

"Don't count on it. He won't be here in time to
help us any—Bigelow'll see to that."

"What will we do?"

"Well, we'll just have to keep Connick from setting this place afire till we can get away from here.
Darkness will help us more than it will those fellows
out there."

Lurelle nodded confidently.

As the day wore on, Mark Connick wasted no more
slugs on the ranch house. There wasn't a gun on the
Bar G powerful enough to penetrate the log walls
from a distance, and those inside would be safe so
long as they kept below the windows and away from
the doors. Noon came. Lurelle wanted to build a fire
in the cookstove and make another pot of coffee,
rustle up some grub. Tolliver wouldn't let her. The
danger of more gunshots from the outbuildings was
too great. They ate canned tomatoes, which also had
to serve them in lieu of drinking water.

A little after twelve, Lurelle wanted to enter her
bedroom for something, so Tolliver went toward
the front of the house, intending to take a look from
her windows, against the possibility of gunfire being

directed at that part of the house. He didn't reach Lurelle's doorway.

Mark Connick stepped out of the living room and took a quick shot at him.

Why? flashed through Tolliver's mind as he hurled himself sidewise against the wall. A cry of terror from Lurelle filled Tolliver's hearing as he went down, with Connick's gun spouting more lead and flame and acrid white smoke at him. Mustached features contorted with hatred, Connick never did hit him although the range was point-blank. Tolliver finally got his own gun out, springing along the floor. Half-erect, he drove three slugs at Connick's middle. He was standing over Connick even as the Circle C owner dropped his six-shooter and clawed wildly at the wall for support. Tolliver watched him until he was flat on his back, his face immobile, eyes glazed.

Glancing down the hall, Tolliver saw Lurelle's hazy outline through the powdersmoke. Voice, seeming loud in the sudden silence, he said, "Are you all right?"

She had her hands over her ears but took them down to ask, "What did you say?"

Obviously she was unhurt, so Tolliver said, "Take a look out and see if the rest of them aren't high-tailing it."

Lurelle didn't move for a couple of seconds.

"Help's coming," Tolliver said. "Sprague's prob-

ably riding up with plenty of backing. Connick
wouldn't have made a try at me before dark otherwise. He hated me so much he couldn't bear the
thought of riding off and leaving me here with
you."

Several horses cantered into the back yard as Tolliver threw a blanket over Connick's body, but when
he went out to stand beside Lurelle on the back gallery, it wasn't Walt Sprague that he saw. Sprague
hadn't come.

Tolliver was looking at Fanny and Cheryl Hashim,
Phillips and Sturdivant. Sheriff Stroud was there,
too, with Bigelow and Hutton and the yellow-haired
man's other riders.

Lurelle had already told them about Dobbs and
Connick.

Sheriff Stroud looked at Tolliver, saying, "Kelse
and Jepsen struck out down the river. Have they
done enough for us to take their trail?"

"Just let them high-tail it, Jim."

"They didn't all run," Stroud said, and gestured at
a couple of hands under the blacksmith shed.

Tolliver said, "They're all right. They're good
men."

"It's all wound up, huh?"

Tolliver nodded. He turned his attention from the
sheriff to Bigelow, who was watching him with bright
speculation.

Bigelow said, "I'm ready to call it even, Tolliver."

"Going back to Devils River?" Tolliver asked. He hoped that Bigelow was leaving, because old Jake Mawson could return when the yellow-haired man left the valley.

"I'm going to sell out down there and throw in with Mrs. Hashim," Bigelow said.

Weather-tanned round face revealing satisfaction, Fanny Hashim said, "From what Lurelle tells us, I need him. Connick won't be squatting on my south range now."

Tolliver was still hearing Bigelow say that he was ready to call it even—something of more importance right now than anything concerning the Muleshoe's lower graze. Giving Bigelow a level look, Tolliver said, "All right, we'll call it square. But don't try to give orders on this side of the river. We'll keep whoever we want to on our payroll, regardless of what you think about him."

Bigelow said in a clipped tone, "I'm not looking for a fight with you."

Sheriff Stroud swung a leg over his saddle cantle. "You fellows all light down, Bigelow, and we'll see what this spread offers in the way of grub."

"Yes," Lurelle said. "You and Cheryl, too, Mrs. Hashim."

Bigelow dismounted at once, ground-hitching his horse. His riders did likewise, and after a session at the pump, they followed the paunchy lawman into the Bar G cookshack. Phillips and Sturdivant kept to their saddles, with Fanny Hashim saying, "We're in a hurry to get home, Lurelle."

"Phil," Tolliver said, "some time when it comes handy, haze my roan across the river."

"Sure will, Tolliver."

Lurelle came off the porch to follow the Muleshoe folks a little ways. She and Mrs. Hashim talked for quite a while. When she returned to the house, Lurelle offered no comment, but Tolliver thought she seemed pleased.

Sheriff Stroud and Bigelow and the others stayed all afternoon, helping Tolliver set the Bar G headquarters to rights. Tolliver had the *remudero* throw the cavvy back onto grass and sent him after his saddle gear. Sheriff Stroud stayed for supper but declined Lurelle's invitation to stay all night.

Lurelle said, "Rufe and I will be getting married right away. Tell Felicia I want her to help me with my wedding."

Stroud said, "She'll sure be tickled to, Lurelle. Ain't nothing she likes better than a good wedding." Before he rode off with the Bigelow outfit leading the horse rented from the Plaza corral, the lawman said privately to Tolliver, "You're shorthanded, but it's a damned good thing for the folks in this whole valley to get shut of Ben's gun-slingers. They wouldn't stand hitched for Connick like they did for Ben, eh?"

"They figured Connick was going to lose."

"Well," Stroud said, "I'll find more hands for you."

"I don't know yet what we're going to do, Sheriff. We may move the Bar G headquarters up to my place."

The badge-toter offered no comment to that and soon rode off, leaving only the cook and the wrangler with Tolliver and Lurelle.

It was after sundown before Tolliver spoke to Lurelle about moving. He was standing with her on the south end of the front veranda, the timber of the river before them and the still-sunlit wall of the Llano Estacado towering in the north.

Lurelle turned her gaze in the opposite direction, toward the Gregory cemetery. "I don't know, Rufe. I'd rather stay here where my people are. There'll be no more trouble; Fanny Hashim and I gave each other our word on that." She drew a long breath. "But I'll do whatever you want to do."

"It's beautiful up there. Peaceful. Wonderful place for a ranching setup."

She moodily considered it.

Never a man to think that life held more than equal amounts of security and menace, Tolliver moved a watchful gaze over the rangeland, and his attention was seized by a rider approaching from the south.

Noticing the horsebacker, too, Lurelle said, "That's Walt Sprague, and he's alone." She looked at Tolliver, eyes widening.

The spade-bearded Bar G hand came on to stop

at the corral gate as usual. By the time Tolliver and Lurelle had turned through the house to join Sprague there, he had stripped the gear off his horse, and the animal was rolling in the dust. Sprague was holding two guns by their barrels when he turned to Tolliver—a six-shooter and a saddle gun.

"Those are mine," Tolliver said puzzledly, and then he lifted an angry gaze. "I gave those to old Jake Mawson. Where did you get them?"

"Up at your place, Tolliver."

Tolliver didn't lift his arms to take the weapons. He started to speak but shut his lips tight. He swallowed with difficulty, his features contorted. "Bigelow hung him up there at my place, didn't he?"

"Uh-huh. That's where the old man had the money buried."

"Some of Bigelow's money?"

Sprague nodded.

"Walt," Lurelle said, "take those guns on to the bunkhouse. Clean up and eat and turn in. You've had a hard day. Hire any hands?"

"I ain't sure yet, Miss Lurelle."

"You'd better make sure. We haven't got any, and you're foreman here now."

"Am I?" Sprague said, highly pleased.

Lurelle turned back toward the ranch house with Tolliver when Sprague walked away. Halfway there, they stopped to face each other. "You won't go gunning for Bigelow, will you?" she asked.

"I don't know."

Looking at him steadily, she said, "Let's stay here. Let's tear down your buildings and clean that place up. Fix him a grave with a headstone and an iron fence and things."

Tolliver took a breath, watching her with furrowed brow. "If you can want to do that for him after he killed your father, I can want to do anything you desire. Sure, we'll stay here. And I won't fight Bigelow."

She glanced away, gravely thoughtful, then met his eyes again to say, "Don't feel bound by a promise. You may have to fight him, because you don't have all the say. I don't want you to run." He touched her arm to walk her on, wanting to say something but not finding the right words. Later, he learned that there were no words for what he was trying to express. Misuse had ruined them.